G K CHESTERTON

Tales of the Long Bow

This edition published in 2001 by House of Stratus, an imprint of Stratus Holdings plc, 24c Old Burlington Street, London, W1X 1RL, UK.

www.houseofstratus.com

Typeset, printed and bound by House of Stratus.

A catalogue record for this book is available from the British Library.

ISBN 0-7551-0021-2

Contents

I

The Unpresentable Appearance of Colonel Crane

These tales concern the doing of things recognized as impossible to do; impossible to believe; and, as the weary reader may well cry aloud, impossible to read about. Did the narrator merely say that they happened, without saying how they happened, they could easily be classified with the cow who jumped over the moon and the more introspective individual who jumped down his own throat. In short, they are all tall stories; and though tall stories may also be true stories, there is something in the very phrase appropriate to such a topsy-turvydom; for the logician will presumably class a tall story with a corpulent epigram or a long-legged essay. It is only proper that such impossible incidents should begin in the most prim and prosaic of all places, at the most prim and prosaic of all times, and apparently with the most prim and prosaic of all human beings.

The place was a straight suburban road of strictly-fenced suburban houses on the outskirts of a modern town. The time was about twenty minutes to eleven on Sunday morning, when a procession of suburban families in Sunday clothes were passing decorously up the road to church. And the man was a very respectable retired military man named Colonel Crane, who was also going to church, as he had done every Sunday at the same hour for a long stretch of years. There was no obvious difference between him and his neighbours, except that he was a little less obvious. His house was only called White Lodge, and was, therefore, less alluring to the romantic passer-by than Rowanmere on the one side or Heatherbrae on the other. He turned out spick and span for church as if for parade; but he was much too well dressed to be pointed out as a well-dressed man. He was quite handsome in a dry, sun-baked style; but his bleached blond hair was a colourless sort that could look either light brown or pale grey; and though his blue eyes were clear, they looked out a little heavily under lowered lids. Colonel Crane was something of a survival. He was not really old; indeed he was barely middle-aged; and had gained his last distinctions in the great war. But a variety of causes had kept him true to the traditional type of the old professional soldier, as it had existed before 1914; when a small parish would have only one colonel as it had only one curate. It would be quite unjust to call him a dug-out; indeed, it would be much truer to call him a dug-in. For he had remained in the traditions as firmly and patiently as he had remained in the trenches. He was simply a man who happened to have no taste for changing his habits, and had never worried about conventions enough to alter them. One of his excellent habits was to go to church at eleven o'clock, and he therefore went there; and did not know that there went with him something of an old-world air and a passage in the history of England.

As he came out of his front door, however, on that particular morning, he was twisting a scrap of paper in his fingers and frowning with somewhat unusual perplexity. Instead of walking straight to his garden gate he walked once or twice up and down his front garden, swinging his black walking-cane. The note had been handed in to him at breakfast, and it evidently involved some practical problem calling for immediate solution. He stood a few minutes with his eye riveted on a red daisy at the corner of the nearest flower-bed; and then a new expression began to work in the muscles of his bronzed face, giving a slightly grim hint of humour, of which few except his intimates were aware. Folding up the paper and putting it into his waistcoat pocket, he strolled round the house to the back garden, behind which was the kitchen garden, in which an old servant, a sort of factotum or handyman, named Archer, was acting as kitchen-gardener.

Archer was also a survival. Indeed, the two had survived together; had survived a number of things that had killed a good many other people. But though they had been together through the war that was also a revolution, and had a complete confidence in each other, the man Archer had never been able to lose the oppressive manners of a manservant. He performed the duties of a gardener with the air of a butler. He really performed the duties very well and enjoyed them very much; perhaps he enjoyed them all the more because he was a clever Cockney, to whom the country crafts were a new hobby. But somehow, whenever he said, "I have put in the seeds, sir," it always sounded like, "I have put the sherry on the table, sir"; and he could not say "Shall I pull the carrots?" without seeming to say, "Would you be requiring the claret?"

"I hope you're not working on Sunday," said the Colonel, with a much more pleasant smile than most people got from him, though he was always polite to everybody. "You're getting too fond of these rural pursuits. You've become a rustic yokel."

"I was venturing to examine the cabbages, sir," replied the rustic yokel, with a painful precision of articulation. "Their condition yesterday evening did not strike me as satisfactory"

"Glad you didn't sit up with them," answered the Colonel. "But it's lucky you're interested in cabbages. I want to talk to you about cabbages."

"About cabbages, sir?" inquired the other respectfully

But the Colonel did not appear to pursue the topic, for he was gazing in sudden abstraction at another object in the vegetable plots in front of him. The Colonel's garden, like the Colonel's house, hat, coat and demeanour, was well-appointed in an unobtrusive fashion; and in the part of it devoted to flowers there dwelt something indefinable that seemed older that the suburbs. The hedges, even, in being as neat as Surbiton managed to look as mellow as Hampton Court, as if their very artificiality belonged rather to Queen Anne than Queen Victoria; and the stone-rimmed pond with a ring of irises somehow looked like a classic pool and not merely an artificial puddle. It is idle to analyse how a man's soul and social type will somehow soak into his surroundings; anyhow, the soul of Mr Archer had sunk into the kitchen garden so as to give it a fine shade of difference. He was after all a practical man, and the practice of his new trade was much more of a real appetite with him than words would suggest. Hence the kitchen garden was not artificial, but autochthonous; it really looked like a corner of a farm in the country; and all sorts of practical devices were set up there. Strawberries were netted-in against the birds; strings were stretched across with feathers fluttering from them; and in the middle of the principal bed stood an ancient and authentic scarecrow. Perhaps the only incongruous intruder, capable of disputing with the scarecrow his rural reign, was the curious boundary-stone which marked the edge of his domain; and which was, in fact, a shapeless South Sea idol, planted there with no more appropriateness than a door-scraper. But Colonel Crane would not have been so complete a type of the old army man if he had not hidden somewhere a hobby connected with his travels. His hobby had at one time been savage folklore; and he had the relic of it on the edge of the kitchen garden. At the moment, however, he was not looking at the idol, but at the scarecrow.

"By the way, Archer," he said, "don't you think the scarecrow wants a new hat?"

"I should hardly think it would be necessary sir," said the gardener gravely

"But look here," said the Colonel, "you must consider the philosophy of scarecrows. In theory, that is supposed to convince some rather simple-minded bird that I am walking in my garden. That thing with the unmentionable hat is Me. A trifle sketchy, perhaps. Sort of impressionist portrait; but hardly likely to impress. Man with a hat like that would never be really firm with a sparrow. Conflict of wills, and all that, and I bet the sparrow would come out on top. By the way what's that stick tied on to it?"

"I believe, sir," said Archer, "that it is supposed to represent a gun."

"Held at a highly unconvincing angle," observed Crane. "Man with a hat like that would be sure to miss."

"Would you desire me to procure another hat?" inquired the patient Archer.

"No, no," answered his master carelessly. "As the poor fellow's got such a rotten hat, I'll give him mine. Like the scene of St Martin and the beggar."

"Give him yours," repeated Archer respectfully, but faintly

The Colonel took off his burnished top hat and gravely placed it on the head of the South Sea idol at his feet. It had a queer effect of bringing the grotesque lump of stone to life, as if a goblin in a top hat was grinning at the garden.

"You think the hat shouldn't be quite new?" he inquired almost anxiously "Not done among the best scarecrows, perhaps. Well, let's see what we can do to mellow it a little."

He whirled up his walking-stick over his head and laid a smacking stroke across the silk hat, smashing it over the hollow eyes of the idol.

"Softened with the touch of time now, I think," he remarked, holding out the silken remnants to the gardener. "Put it on the scarecrow, my friend; I don't want it. You can bear witness it's no use to me."

Archer obeyed like an automaton, an automaton with rather round eyes.

"We must hurry up," said the Colonel cheerfully "I was early for church, but I'm afraid I'm a bit late now."

"Did you propose to attend church without a hat, sir?" asked the other.

"Certainly not. Most irreverent," said the Colonel. "Nobody should neglect to remove his hat on entering church. Well, if I haven't got a hat, I shall neglect to remove it. Where is your reasoning power this morning? No, no, just dig up one of your cabbages."

Once more the well-trained servant managed to repeat the word "Cabbages" with his own strict accent; but in its constriction there was a hint of strangulation.

"Yes, go and pull up a cabbage, there's a good fellow," said the Colonel. "I must really be getting along; I believe I heard it strike eleven."

Mr Archer moved heavily in the direction of the plot of cabbages, which swelled with monstrous contours and many colours; objects, perhaps, more worthy of the philosophic eye than is taken into account by the more flippant of tongue. Vegetables are curious-looking things and less commonplace than they sound. If we called a cabbage a cactus, or some such queer name, we might see it as an equally queer thing.

These philosophical truths did the Colonel reveal by anticipating the dubious Archer, and dragging a great, green cabbage with its trailing root out of the earth. He then picked up a sort of pruning-knife and cut short the long tail of the root; scooped out the inside leaves so as to make a sort of hollow, and gravely reversing it, placed it on his head. Napoleon and other military princes have crowned themselves; and he, like the Caesars, wore a wreath that was, after all, made of green leaves or vegetation. Doubtless there are other comparisons that might occur to any philosophical historian who should look at it in the abstract.

The people going to church certainly looked at it; but they did not look at it in the abstract. To them it appeared singularly concrete; and indeed incredibly solid. The inhabitants of Rowanmere and Heatherbrae followed the Colonel as he strode almost jauntily up the road, with feelings that no philosophy could for the moment meet. There seemed to be nothing to be said, except that one of the most respectable and respected of their neighbours, one who might even be called in a quiet way a pattern of good form if not a leader of fashion, was walking solemnly up to church with a cabbage on the top of his head.

There was indeed no corporate action to meet the crisis. Their world was not one in which a crowd can collect to shout, and still less to jeer. No rotten eggs could be collected from their tidy breakfast tables; and they were not of the sort to throw cabbage stalks at the cabbage. Perhaps there was just that amount of truth in the pathetically picturesque names on their front gates, names suggestive of mountains and mighty lakes concealed somewhere on the premises. It was true that in one sense such a house was a hermitage. Each of these men lived alone and they could not be made into a mob. For miles around there was no public house and no public opinion.

As the Colonel approached the church porch and prepared reverently to remove his vegetarian headgear, he was hailed in a tone a little more hearty than the humane civility that was the slender bond of that society. He returned the greeting without embarrassment, and paused a moment as the man who had spoken to him plunged into further speech. He was a young doctor named Horace Hunter, tall, handsomely dressed, and confident in manner; and though his features were rather plain and his hair rather red, he was considered to have a certain fascination.

"Good morning, Colonel," said the doctor in his resounding tones, "what a f— what a fine day it is."

Stars turned from their courses like comets, so to speak, and the world swerved into wilder possibilities, at that crucial moment when Dr Hunter corrected himself and said, "What a fine day!" instead of "What a funny hat!"

As to why he corrected himself, a true picture of what passed through his mind might sound rather fanciful in itself. It would be less than explicit to say he did so because of a long grey car waiting outside the White Lodge. It might not be a complete explanation to say it was due to a lady walking on stilts at a garden party. Some obscurity might remain, even if we said that it had something to do with a soft shirt and a nickname; nevertheless all these things mingled in the medical gentleman's mind when he made his hurried decision. Above all, it might or might not be sufficient explanation to say that Horace Hunter was a very ambitious young man, that the ring in his voice and the confidence in his manner came from a very simple resolution to rise in the world, and that the world in question was rather worldly.

He liked to be seen talking so confidently to Colonel Crane on that Sunday parade. Crane was comparatively poor, but he knew People. And people who knew People knew what People were doing now; whereas people who didn't know People could only wonder what in the world People would do next. A lady who came with the Duchess when she opened the Bazaar had nodded to Crane and said, "Hullo, Stork," and the doctor had deduced that it was a sort of family joke and not a momentary ornithological confusion. And it was the Duchess who had started all that racing on stilts, which the Vernon-Smiths had introduced at Heatherbrae. But it would have been devilish awkward not to have known what Mrs Vernon-Smith meant when she said, "Of course you stilt." You never knew what they would start next. He remembered how he himself had thought the first man in a soft shirt-front was some funny fellow from nowhere; and then he had begun to see others here and there, and had found that it was not a *faux pas*, but a fashion. It was odd to imagine he would ever begin to see vegetable hats here and there, but you never could tell; and he wasn't going to make the same mistake again. His first medical impulse had been to add to the Colonel's fancy costume with a strait-waistcoat. But Crane did not look like a lunatic, and certainly did not look like a man playing a practical joke. He had not the stiff and self-conscious solemnity of the joker. He took it quite naturally. And one thing was certain: if it really was the latest thing, the doctor must take it as naturally as the Colonel did. So he said it was a fine day, and was gratified to learn that there was no disagreement on that question.

The doctor's dilemma, if we may apply the phrase, had been the whole neighbourhood's dilemma. The doctor's decision was also the whole neighbourhood's decision. It was not so much that most of the good people there shared in Hunter's serious social ambitions, but rather that they were naturally prone to negative and cautious decisions. They lived in a delicate dread of being interfered with; and they were just enough to apply the principle by not interfering with other people. They had also a subconscious sense that the mild and respectable military gentleman would not be altogether an easy person to interfere with. The consequence was that the Colonel carried his monstrous green headgear about the streets of that suburb for nearly a week, and nobody ever mentioned the subject to him. It was about the end of that time (while the doctor had been scanning the horizon for aristocrats crowned with cabbage, and, not seeing any, was summoning his natural impudence to speak) that the final interruption came; and with the interruption the explanation.

The Colonel had every appearance of having forgotten all about the hat. He took it off and on like any other hat; he hung it on the hat-peg in his narrow front hall where there was nothing else but his sword hung on two hooks and an old brown map of the seventeenth century. He handed it to Archer when that correct character seemed to insist on his official right to hold it; he did not insist on his official right to brush it, for fear it should fall to pieces; but he occasionally gave it a cautious shake, accompanied by a look of restrained distaste. But the Colonel himself never had any appearance of either liking or disliking it. The unconventional thing had already become one of his conventions – the conventions which he never considered enough to violate. It is probable, therefore, that what ultimately took place was as much of a surprise to him as to anybody. Anyhow, the explanation, or explosion, came in the following fashion.

Mr Vernon-Smith, the mountaineer whose foot was on his native heath at Heatherbrae, was a small, dapper gentleman with a big-bridged nose, dark moustache, and dark eyes with a settled expression of anxiety, though nobody knew what there was to be anxious about in his very solid social existence. He was a friend of Dr Hunter; one might almost say a humble friend. For he had the negative snobbishness that could only admire the positive and progressive snobbishness of that soaring and social figure. A man like Dr Hunter likes to have a man like Mr Smith, before whom he can pose as a perfect man of the world. What appears more extraordinary, a man like Mr Smith really likes to have a man like Dr Hunter to pose at him and swagger over him and snub him. Anyhow, Vernon-Smith had ventured to hint that the new hat of his neighbour Crane was not of a pattern familiar in every fashion-plate. And Dr Hunter, bursting with the secret of his own original diplomacy, had snubbed the suggestion and snowed it under with frosty scorn. With shrewd, resolute gestures, with large allusive phrases, he had left on his friend's mind the impression that the whole social world would dissolve if a word were said on so delicate a topic. Mr Vernon-Smith formed a general idea that the Colonel would explode with a loud bang at the very vaguest allusion to vegetables, or the most harmless adumbration or verbal shadow of a hat. As usually happens in such cases, the words he was forbidden to say repeated themselves perpetually in his mind with the rhythmic pressure of a pulse. It was his temptation at the moment to call all houses hats and all visitors vegetables.

When Crane came out of his front gate that morning he found his neighbour Vernon-Smith standing outside, between the spreading laburnum and the lamp-post, talking to a young lady, a distant cousin of his family. This girl was an art student on her own – a little too much on her own for the standards of Heatherbrae, and, therefore (some would infer), yet further beyond those of White Lodge. Her brown hair was bobbed, and the Colonel did not admire bobbed hair. On the other hand, she had a rather attractive face, with honest brown eyes a little too wide apart, which diminished the impression of beauty but increased the impression of honesty. She also had a very fresh and unaffected voice, and the Colonel had often heard it calling out scores at tennis on the other side of the garden wall. In some vague sort of way it made him feel old; at least, he was not sure whether he felt older than he was, or younger than he ought to be. It was not until they met under the lamp-post that he knew her name was Audrey Smith; and he was faintly thankful for the single monosyllable. Mr Vernon-Smith presented her, and very nearly said: "May I introduce my cabbage?" instead of "my cousin."

The Colonel, with unaffected dullness, said it was a fine day; and his neighbour, rallying from his last narrow escape, continued the talk with animation. His manner, as when he poked his big nose and beady black eyes into local meetings and committees, was at once hesitating and emphatic.

"This young lady is going in for Art," he said; "a poor look-out, isn't it? I expect we shall see her drawing in chalk on the paving stones and expecting us to throw a penny into the – into a tray, or something." Here he dodged another danger. "But, of course, she thinks she's going to be an RA."

"I hope not," said the young woman hotly. "Pavement artists are much more honest than most of the RA's."

"I wish those friends of yours didn't give you such revolutionary ideas," said Mr Vernon-Smith. "My cousin knows the most dreadful cranks, vegetarians and – and Socialists." He chanced it, feeling that vegetarians were not quite the same as vegetables; and he felt sure the Colonel would share his horror of Socialists. "People who want us to be equal, and all that. What I say is – we're not equal and we never can be. As I always say to Audrey – if all the property were divided tomorrow, it would go back into the same hands. It's a law of nature, and if a man thinks he can get round a law of nature, why he's talking through his – I mean, he's as mad as a – "

Recoiling from the omnipresent image, he groped madly in his mind for the alternative of a March hare. But before he could find it, the girl had cut in and completed his sentence. She smiled serenely, and said in her clear and ringing tones:

"As mad as Colonel Crane's hatter."

It is not unjust to Mr Vernon-Smith to say that he fled as from a dynamite explosion. It would be unjust to say that he deserted a lady in distress, for she did not look in the least like a distressed lady, and he himself was a very distressed gentleman. He attempted to wave her indoors with some wild pretext, and eventually vanished there himself with an equally random apology. But the other two took no notice of him; they continued to confront each other, and both were smiling.

"I think you must be the bravest man in England," she said. "I don't mean anything about the war, or the DSO and all that; I mean about this. Oh, yes, I do know a little about you, but there's one thing I don't know. Why do you do it?"

"I think it is you who are the bravest woman in England," he answered, "or, at any rate, the bravest person in these parts. I've walked about this town for a week, feeling like the last fool in creation, and expecting somebody to say something. And not a soul has said a word. They seem all to be afraid of saying the wrong thing."

"I think they're deadly," observed Miss Smith. "And if they don't have cabbages for hats, it's only because they have turnips for heads."

"No," said the Colonel gently; "I have many generous and friendly neighbours here, including your cousin. Believe me, there is a case for conventions, and the world is wiser than you know. You are too young not to be intolerant. But I can see you've got the fighting spirit; that is the best part of youth and intolerance. When you said that word just now, by Jove you looked like Britomart."

"She is the Militant Suffragette in the Faerie Queene, isn't she?" answered the girl. "I'm afraid I don't know my English literature as well as you do. You see, I'm an artist, or trying to be one; and some people say that narrows a person. But I can't help getting cross with all the varnished vulgarity they talk about everything – look at what he said about Socialism."

"It was a little superficial," said Crane with a smile.

"And that," she concluded, "is why I admire your hat, though I don't know why you wear it."

This trivial conversation had a curious effect on the Colonel. There went with it a sort of warmth and a sense of crisis that he had not known since the war. A sudden purpose formed itself in his mind, and he spoke like one stepping across a frontier.

"Miss Smith," he said, "I wonder if I might ask you to pay me a further compliment. It may be unconventional, but I believe you do not stand on these conventions. An old friend of mine will be calling on me shortly to wind up the rather unusual business or ceremonial of which you have chanced to see a part. If you would do me the honour to lunch with me tomorrow at half-past one, the true story of the cabbage awaits you. I promise that you shall hear the real reason. I might even say I promise you shall see the real reason."

"Why, of course I will," said the unconventional one heartily. "Thanks awfully."

The Colonel took an intense interest in the appointments of the luncheon next day. With subconscious surprise he found himself not only interested, but excited. Like many of his type, he took a pleasure in doing such things well, and knew his way about in wine and cookery. But that would not alone explain his pleasure. For he knew that young women generally know very little about wine, and emancipated young women possibly least of all. And though he meant the cookery to be good, he knew that in one feature it would appear rather fantastic. Again, he was a good-natured gentleman who would always have liked young people to enjoy a luncheon party, as he would have liked a child to enjoy a Christmas tree. But there seemed no reason why he should be restless and expectant about it, as if he were a child himself. There was no reason why he should have a sort of happy insomnia, like a child on Christmas Eve. There was really no excuse for his pacing up and down the garden with his cigar, smoking furiously far into the night. For as he gazed at the purple irises and the grey pool in the faint moonshine, something in his feelings passed as if from the one tint to the other; he had a new and unexpected reaction. For the first time he really hated the masquerade he had made himself endure. He wished he could smash the cabbage as he had smashed the top-hat. He was little more than forty years old; but he had never realized how much there was of what was dried and faded about his flippancy till he felt unexpectedly swelling within him the monstrous and solemn vanity of a young man. Sometimes he looked up at the picturesque, the too picturesque, outline of the villa next door, dark against the moonrise, and thought he heard faint voices in it, and something like a laugh.

The visitor who called on the Colonel next morning may have been an old friend, but he was certainly an odd contrast. He was a very abstracted, rather untidy man in a rusty knicker-bocker suit; he had a long head with straight hair of the dark red called auburn, one or two wisps of which stood on end however he brushed it, and a long face, clean-shaven and heavy about the jaw and chin, which he had a way of sinking and settling squarely into his cravat. His name was Hood, and he was apparently a lawyer, though he had not come on strictly legal business. Anyhow, he exchanged greetings with Crane with a quiet warmth and gratification, smiled at the old manservant as if he were an old joke, and showed every sign of an appetite for his luncheon.

The appointed day was singularly warm and bright and everything in the garden seemed to glitter; the goblin god of the South Seas seemed really to grin; and the scarecrow really to have a new hat. The irises round the pool were swinging and flapping in a light breeze; and he remembered they were called "flags" and thought of purple banners going into battle.

She had come suddenly round the corner of the house. Her dress was of a dark but vivid blue, very plain and angular in outline, but not outrageously artistic; and in the morning light she looked less like a schoolgirl and more like a serious woman of twenty-five or thirty; a little older and a great deal more interesting. And something in this morning seriousness increased the reaction of the night before. One single wave of thanksgiving went up from Crane to think that at least his grotesque green hat was gone and done with for ever. He had worn it for a week without caring a curse for anybody; but during that ten minutes' trivial talk under the lamp-post, he felt as if he had suddenly grown donkey's ears in the street.

He had been induced by the sunny weather to have a little table laid for three in a sort of veranda open to the garden. When the three sat down to it, he looked across at the lady and said: "I fear I must exhibit myself as a crank; one of those cranks your cousin disapproves of, Miss Smith. I hope it won't spoil this little lunch for anybody else. But I am going to have a vegetarian meal."

"Are you?" she said. "I should never have said you looked like a vegetarian."

"Just lately I have only looked like a fool," he said dispassionately; "but I think I'd sooner look a fool than a vegetarian in the ordinary way. This is rather a special occasion. Perhaps my friend Hood had better begin; it's really his story more than mine."

"My name is Robert Owen Hood," said that gentleman, rather sardonically. "That's how improbable reminiscences often begin; but the only point now is that my old friend here insulted me horribly by calling me Robin Hood."

"I should have called it a compliment," answered Audrey Smith. "But why did he call you Robin Hood?"

"Because I drew the long bow," said the lawyer.

"But to do you justice," said the Colonel, "it seems that you hit the bull's eye."

As he spoke Archer came in bearing a dish which he placed before his master. He had already served the others with the earlier courses, but he carried this one with the pomp of one bringing the boar's head at Christmas. It consisted of a plain boiled cabbage.

"I was challenged to do something," went on Hood, "which my friend here declared to be impossible. In fact, any sane man would have declared it to be impossible. But I did it for all that. Only my friend, in the heat of rejecting and ridiculing the notion, made use of a hasty expression. I might almost say he made a rash vow."

"My exact words were," said Colonel Crane solemnly: " 'If you can do that, I'll eat my hat.' "

He leaned forward thoughtfully and began to eat it. Then he resumed in the same reflective way:

"You see, all rash vows are verbal or nothing. There might be a debate about the logical and literal way in which my friend Hood fulfilled *his* rash vow. But I put it to myself in the same pedantic sort of way. It wasn't possible to eat any hat that I wore. But it might be possible to wear a hat that I could eat. Articles of dress could hardly be used for diet; but articles of diet could really be used for dress. It seemed to me that I might fairly be said to have made it my hat, if I wore it systematically as a hat and had no other, putting up with all the disadvantages. Making a blasted fool of myself was the fair price to be paid for the vow or wager; for one ought always to lose something on a wager."

And he rose from the table with a gesture of apology.

The girl stood up. "I think it's perfectly splendid," she said. "It's as wild as one of those stories about looking for the Holy Grail."

The lawyer also had risen, rather abruptly, and stood stroking his long chin with his thumb and looking at his old friend under bent brows in a rather reflective manner.

"Well, you've subpoena'd me as a witness all right," he said, "and now, with the permission of the court, I'll leave the witness-box. I'm afraid I must be going. I've got important business at home. Goodbye, Miss Smith."

The girl returned his farewell a little mechanically; and Crane seemed to recover suddenly from a similar trance as he stepped after the retreating figure of his friend.

"I say, Owen," he said hastily, "I'm sorry you're leaving so early. Must you really go?"

"Yes," replied Owen Hood gravely. "My private affairs are quite real and practical, I assure you." His grave mouth worked a little humorously at the corners as he added: "The truth is, I don't think I mentioned it, but I'm thinking of getting married."

"Married!" repeated the Colonel, as if thunderstruck.

"Thanks for your compliments and congratulations, old fellow," said the satiric Mr Hood. "Yes, it's all been thought out. I've even decided whom I am going to marry. She knows about it herself. She has been warned."

"I really beg your pardon," said the Colonel in great distress, "of course I congratulate you most heartily; and her even more heartily. Of course I'm delighted to hear it. The truth is, I was surprised…not so much in that way…"

"Not so much in what way?" asked Hood. "I suppose you mean some would say I am on the way to be an old bachelor. But I've discovered it isn't half so much a matter of years as of ways. Men like me get elderly more by choice than chance; and there's much more choice and less chance in life than your modern fatalists make out. For such people fatalism falsifies even chronology. They're not unmarried because they're old. They're old because they're unmarried."

"Indeed you are mistaken," said Crane earnestly. "As I say, I was surprised, but my surprise was not so rude as you think. It wasn't that I thought there was anything unfitting about... somehow it was rather the other way…as if things could fit better than one thought…as if – but anyhow, little as I know about it, I really do congratulate you."

"I'll tell you all about it before long," replied his friend. "It's enough to say just now that it was all bound up with my succeeding after all in doing – what I did. She was the inspiration, you know. I have done what is called an impossible thing; but believe me, she is really the impossible part of it."

"Well, I must not keep you from such an impossible engagement," said Crane smiling. "Really, I'm confoundedly glad to hear about all this. Well, goodbye for the present."

Colonel Crane stood watching the square shoulders and russet mane of his old friend, as they disappeared down the road, in a rather indescribable state of mind. As he turned hastily back towards his garden and his other guest, he was conscious of a change; things seemed different in some light-headed and illogical fashion. He could not himself trace the connexion; indeed, he did not know whether it was a connexion or a disconnexion. He was very far from being a fool; but his brains were of the sort that are directed outwards to things; the brains of the soldier or the scientific man; and he had no practice in analysing his own mind. He did not quite understand why the news about Owen Hood should give him that dazed sense of a difference in things in general. Doubtless he was very fond of Owen Hood; but he had been fond of other people who had got married without especially disturbing the atmosphere of his own back garden. He even dimly felt that mere affection might have worked the other way; that it might have made him worry about Hood, and wonder whether Hood was making a fool of himself, or even feel suspicious or jealous of Mrs Hood – if there had not been something else that made him feel quite the other way. He could not quite understand it; there seemed to be an increasing number of things that he could not understand. This world in which he himself wore garlands of green cabbage and in which his old friend the lawyer got married suddenly like a man going mad – this world was a new world, at once fresh and frightening, in which he could hardly understand the figures that were walking about, even his own. The flowers in the flowerpots had a new look about them, at once bright and nameless; and even the line of vegetables beyond could not altogether depress him with the memories of recent levity. Had he indeed been a prophet, or a visionary seeing the future, he might have seen that green line of cabbages extending infinitely like a green sea to the horizon. For he stood at the beginning of a story which was not to terminate until his incongruous cabbage had come to mean something that he had never meant by it. That green patch was to spread like a great green conflagration almost to the ends of the earth. But he was a practical person and the very reverse of a prophet; and like many other practical persons, he often did things without very clearly knowing what he was doing. He had the innocence of some patriarch or primitive hero in the morning of the world, founding more than he could himself realize of his legend and his line. Indeed he felt very much like somebody in the morning of the world; but beyond that he could grasp nothing.

Audrey Smith was standing not so very many yards away; for it was only for a few strides that he had followed his elder guest towards the gate. Yet her figure had fallen far enough back out of the foreground to take on the green framework of the garden; so that her dress might almost have been blue with a shade of distance. And when she spoke to him, even from that little way off, her voice took on inevitably a new suggestion of one calling out familiarly and from afar, as one calls to an old companion. It moved him in a disproportionate fashion, though all that she said was:

"What became of your old hat?"

"I lost it," he replied gravely, "obviously I had to lose it. I believe the scarecrow found it."

"Oh, do let's go and look at the scarecrow," she cried.

He led her without a word to the kitchen garden and gravely explained each of its outstanding features; from the serious Mr Archer resting on his spade to the grotesque South Sea Island god grinning at the corner of the plot. He spoke as with an increasing solemnity and verbosity, and all the time knew little or nothing of what he said.

At last she cut into his monologue with an abstraction that was almost rude; yet her brown eyes were bright and her sympathy undisguised.

"Don't talk about it," she cried with illogical enthusiasm. "It looks as if we were really right in the middle of the country. It's as unique as the Garden of Eden. It's simply the most delightful place – "

It was at this moment, for some unaccountable reason, that the Colonel who had lost his hat suddenly proceeded to lose his head. Standing in that grotesque vegetable scenery, a black and stiff yet somehow stately figure, he proceeded in the most traditional manner to offer the lady everything he possessed, not forgetting the scarecrow or the cabbages; a half-humourous memory of which returned to him with the boomerang of bathos.

"When I think of the encumbrances on the estate–" he concluded gloomily. "Well, there they are; a scarecrow and a cannibal fetish and a stupid man who has stuck in a rut of respectability and conventional ways."

"Very conventional," she said, "especially in his taste in hats."

"That was the exception, I'm afraid," he said earnestly. "You'd find those things very rare and most things very dull. I can't help having fallen in love with you; but for all that we are in different worlds; and you belong to a younger world, which says what it thinks, and cannot see what most of our silences and our scruples meant."

"I suppose we are very rude," she said thoughtfully, "and you must certainly excuse me if I do say what I think."

"I deserve no better," he replied mournfully.

"Well, I think I must be in love with you too," she replied calmly. "I don't see what time has to do with being fond of people. You are the most original person I ever knew."

"My dear, my dear," he protested almost brokenly, "I fear you are making a mistake. Whatever else I am, I never set up to be original."

"You must remember," she replied, "that I have known a good many people who did set up to be original. An Art School swarms with them; and there are any number among those socialist and vegetarian friends of mine you were talking about. They would think nothing of wearing cabbages on their heads, of course. Any one of them would be capable of getting inside a pumpkin if he could. Any one of them might appear in public dressed entirely in watercress. But that's just it. They might well wear watercress for they are water-creatures; they go with the stream. They do those things because those things are done; because they are done in their own Bohemian set.

Unconventionality is their convention. I don't mind it myself; I think it's great fun; but that doesn't mean that I don't know real strength or independence when I see it. All that is just molten and formless; but the really strong man is one who can make a mould and then break it. When a man like you can suddenly do a thing like that, after twenty years of habit, for the sake of his word, then somehow one really does feel that man is man and master of his fate."

"I doubt if I am master of my fate," replied Crane, "and I do not know whether I ceased to be yesterday or two minutes ago."

He stood there for a moment like a man in heavy armour. Indeed, the antiquated image is not inappropriate in more ways than one. The new world within him was so alien from the whole habit in which he lived, from the very gait and gestures of his daily life, conducted through countless days, that his spirit had striven before it broke its shell. But it was also true that even if he could have done what every man wishes to do at such a moment, something supreme and satisfying, it would have been something in a sense formal or it would not have satisfied him. He was one of those to whom it is natural to be ceremonial. Even the music in his mind, too deep and distant for him to catch or echo, was the music of old and ritual dances and not of revelry; and it was not for nothing that he had built gradually about him that garden of the grey stone fountain and the great hedge of yew. He bent suddenly and kissed her hand.

"I like that," she said. "You ought to have powdered hair and a sword."

"I apologize," he said gravely, "no modern man is worthy of you. But indeed I fear, in every sense I am not a very modern man."

"You must never wear that hat again," she said, indicating the battered original topper.

"To tell the truth," he observed mildly "I had not any intention of resuming that one."

"Silly," she said briefly, "I don't mean that hat; I mean that sort of hat. As a matter of fact, there couldn't be a finer hat than the cabbage."

"My dear – " he protested; but she was looking at him quite seriously.

"I told you I was an artist, and didn't know much about literature," she said. "Well, do you know it really does make a difference. Literary people let words get between them and things. We do at least look at the things and not the names of the things. You think a cabbage is comic because the name sounds comic and even vulgar; something between 'cab' and 'garbage,' I suppose. But a cabbage isn't really comic or vulgar. You wouldn't think so if you simply had to paint it. Haven't you seen Dutch and Flemish galleries, and don't you know what great men painted cabbages? What they saw was certain lines and colours; very wonderful lines and colours."

"It may be all very well in a picture," he began doubtfully.

She suddenly laughed aloud.

"You idiot," she cried; "don't you know you looked perfectly splendid? The curves were like a great turban of leaves and the root rose like the spike of a helmet; it was rather like the turbaned helmets on some of Rembrandt's figures, with the face like bronze in the shadows of green and purple. That's the sort of thing artists can see, who keep their eyes and heads clear of words! And then you want to apologize for not wearing that stupid stove-pipe covered with blacking, when you went about wearing a coloured crown like a king. And you were like a king in this country; for they were all afraid of you."

As he continued a faint protest, her laughter took on a more mischievous shade. "If you'd stuck to it a little longer, I swear they'd all have been wearing vegetables for hats. I swear I saw my cousin the other day standing with a sort of trowel, and looking irresolutely at a cabbage."

Then, after a pause, she said with a beautiful irrelevancy:

"What was it Mr Hood did that you said he couldn't do?"

But these are tales of topsy-turvydom even in the sense that they have to be told tail-foremost. And he who would know the answer to that question must deliver himself up to the intolerable tedium of reading the story of The Improbable Success of Mr Owen Hood, and an interval must be allowed him before such torments are renewed.

II

The Improbable Success of Mr Owen Hood

Heroes who have endured the heavy labour of reading to the end the story of The Unpresentable Appearance of Colonel Crane are aware that his achievement was the first of a series of feats counted impossible, like the quests of the Arthurian knights. For the purpose of this tale, in which the Colonel is but a secondary figure, it is enough to say that he was long known and respected, before his last escapade, as a respectable and retired military man in a residential part of Surrey, with a sunburnt complexion and an interest in savage mythology. As a fact, however, he had gathered the sunburn and the savage myths some time before he had managed to collect the respectability and the suburban residence. In his early youth he had been a traveller of the adventurous and even restless sort; and he only concerns this story because he was a member of a sort of club or clique of young men whose adventurousness verged on extravagance. They were all eccentrics of one kind or another, some professing extreme revolutionary and some extreme reactionary opinions, and some both. Among the latter may be classed Mr Robert Owen Hood, the somewhat unlegal lawyer who is the hero of this tale.

Robert Owen Hood was Crane's most intimate and incongruous friend. Hood was from the first as sedentary as Crane was adventurous. Hood was to the end as casual as Crane was conventional. The prefix of Robert Owen was a relic of a vague revolutionary tradition in his family; but he inherited along with it a little money that allowed him to neglect the law and cultivate a taste for liberty and for drifting and dreaming in lost corners of the country, especially in the little hills between the Severn and the Thames. In the upper reaches of the latter river is an islet in which he loved especially to sit fishing, a shabby but not commonplace figure clad in grey, with a mane of rust-coloured hair and a long face with a large chin, rather like Napoleon. Beside him, on the occasion now in question, stood the striking contrast of his alert military friend in full travelling kit; being on the point of starting for one of his odysseys in the South Seas.

"Well," demanded the impatient traveller in a tone of remonstrance, "have you caught anything?"

"You once asked me," replied the angler placidly, "what I meant by calling you a materialist. That is what I meant by calling you a materialist."

"If one must be a materialist or a madman," snorted the soldier, "give me materialism."

"On the contrary," replied his friend, "your fad is far madder than mine. And I doubt if it's any more fruitful. The moment men like you see a man sitting by a river with a rod, they are insanely impelled to ask him what he has caught. But when you go off to shoot big game, as you call it, nobody asks you what you have caught. Nobody expects you to bring home a hippopotamus for supper. Nobody has ever seen you walking up Pall Mall, followed respectfully by a captive giraffe. Your bag of elephants, though enormous, seems singularly unobtrusive; left in the cloakroom, no doubt. Personally, I doubt if you ever catch anything. It's all decorously hidden in desert sand and dust and distance. But what I catch is something far more elusive, and as slippery as any fish. It is the soul of England."

"I should think you'd catch a cold if not a fish," answered Crane, "sitting dangling your feet in a pool like that. I like to move about a little more. Dreaming is all very well in its way."

At this point a symbolic cloud ought to have come across the sun, and a certain shadow of mystery and silence must rest for a moment upon the narrative. For it was at this moment that James Crane, being blind with inspiration, uttered his celebrated Prophecy, upon which this improbable narrative turns. As was commonly the case with men uttering omens, he was utterly unconscious of anything ominous about what he said. A moment after he would probably not know that he had said it. A moment after, it was as if a cloud of strange shape had indeed passed from the face of the sun.

The prophecy has taken the form of a proverb. In due time the patient, all-suffering reader, may learn what proverb. As it happened, indeed, the conversation had largely consisted of proverbs; as is often the case with men like Hood, whose hearts are with that old English country life from which all the proverbs came. But it was Crane who said:

"It's all very well to be fond of England; but a man who wants to help England mustn't let the grass grow under his feet."

"And that's just what I want to do," answered Hood. "That's exactly what even your poor tired people in big towns really want to do. When a wretched clerk walks down Threadneedle Street, wouldn't he really be delighted if he could look down and see the grass growing under his feet; a magic green carpet in the middle of the pavement? It would be like a fairy-tale."

"Well, but he wouldn't sit like a stone as you do," replied the other. "A man might let the grass grow under his feet without actually letting the ivy grow up his legs. That sounds like a fairy-tale, too, if you like, but there's no proverb to recommend it."

"Oh, there are proverbs on my side, if you come to that," answered Hood laughing. "I might remind you about the rolling stone that gathers no moss."

"Well, who wants to gather moss except a few fussy old ladies?" demanded Crane. "Yes, I'm a rolling stone, I suppose; and I go rolling round the earth as the earth goes rolling round the sun. But I'll tell you what; there's one kind of stone that does really gather moss."

"And what is that, my rambling geologist?"

"A gravestone," said Crane.

There was a silence, and Hood sat gazing with his owlish face at the dim pools in which the dark woods were mirrored. At last he said:

"Moss isn't the only thing found on that. Sometimes there is the word *Resurgam*."

"Well, I hope you will," said Crane genially. "But the trumpet will have to be pretty loud to wake you up. It's my opinion you'll be too late for the Day of Judgment."

"Now if this were a true dramatic dialogue," remarked Hood, "I should answer that it would be better for you if you were. But it hardly seems a Christian sentiment for a parting. Are you really off today?"

"Yes, tonight," replied his friend. "Sure you won't come with me to the Cannibal Islands?"

"I prefer my own island," said Mr Owen Hood.

When his friend had gone he continued to gaze abstractedly at the tranquil topsy-turvydom in the green mirror of the pool, nor did he change his posture and hardly moved his head. This might be partly explained by the still habits of a fisherman; but to tell the truth, it was not easy to discover whether the solitary lawyer really wanted to catch any fish. He often carried a volume of Isaac Walton in his pocket, having a love of the old English literature as of the old English landscape. But if he was an angler, he certainly was not a very complete angler.

But the truth is that Owen Hood had not been quite candid with his friend about the spell that held him to that particular islet in the Upper Thames. If he had said, as he was quite capable of saying, that he expected to catch the miraculous draught of fishes or the whale that swallowed Jonah, or even the great sea-serpent, his expressions would have been merely symbolical. But they would have been the symbol of something as unique and unattainable. For Mr Owen Hood was really fishing for something that very few fishermen ever catch; and that was a dream of his boyhood, and something that had happened on that lonely spot long ago.

Years before, when he was a very young man, he had sat fishing on that island one evening as the twilight turned to dark, and two or three broad bands of silver were all that was left of the sunset behind the darkening trees. The birds were dropping out of the sky and there was no noise except the soft noises of the river. Suddenly and without a sound, as comes a veritable vision, a girl had come out of the woods opposite. She spoke to him across the stream, asking him he hardly knew what, which he answered he hardly knew how. She was dressed in white and carried a bunch of bluebells loose in her hand; her hair in a straight fringe of gold was low on her forehead; she was pale like ivory, and her pale eyelids had a sort of flutter as of nervous emotion. There came on him a strangling sense of stupidity. But he must have managed to speak civilly, for she lingered; and he must have said something to amuse her, for she laughed. Then followed the incident he could never analyse, though he was an introspective person. Making a gesture towards something, she managed to drop her loose blue flowers into the water. He knew not what sort of whirlwind was in his head, but it seemed to him that prodigious things were happening, as in an epic of the gods, of which all visible things were but the small signs. Before he knew where he was he was standing dripping on the other bank; for he had splashed in somehow and saved the bunch as if it had been a baby drowning. Of all the things she said he could recall one sentence, that repeated itself perpetually in his mind: "You'll catch your death of cold."

He only caught the cold and not the death; yet even the notion of the latter did not somehow seem disproportionate. The doctor, to whom he was forced to give some sort of explanation of his immersion, was much interested in the story, or what he heard of it, having a pleasure in working out the pedigrees of the county families and the relationships of the best houses in the neighbourhood. By some rich process of elimination he deduced that the lady must be Miss Elizabeth Seymour from Marley Court. The doctor spoke with a respectful relish of such things; he was a rising young practitioner named Hunter, afterwards a neighbour of Colonel Crane. He shared Hood's admiration for the local landscape, and said it was owing to the beautiful way in which Marley Court was kept up.

"It's landowners like that," he said, "who have made England. It's all very well for Radicals to talk; but where should we be without the landowners?"

"Oh, I'm all for landowners," said Hood rather wearily. "I like them so much I should like more of them. More and more landowners. Hundreds and thousands of them."

It is doubtful whether Dr Hunter quite followed his enthusiasm, or even his meaning; but Hood had reason later to remember this little conversation; so far as he was in a mood to remember any conversations except one.

Anyhow, it was vain to disguise from the intelligent though exhausted reader that this was probably the true origin of Mr Hood's habit of sitting solidly on that island and gazing abstractedly at that bank. All through the years when he felt his first youth was passing, and even when he seemed to be drifting towards middle age, he haunted that valley like a ghost, waiting for something that never came again. It is by no means certain, in the last and most subtle analysis, that he even expected it to come again. Somehow it seemed too like a miracle for that. Only this place had become the shrine of the miracle; and he felt that if anything ever did happen there, he must be there to see. And so it came about that he was there to see when things did happen; and rather queer things had happened before the end.

One morning he saw an extraordinary thing. That indeed would not have seemed extraordinary to most people; but it was quite apocalyptic to him. A dusty man came out of the woods carrying what looked like dusty pieces of timber, and proceeded to erect on the bank what turned out to be a sort of hoarding, a very large wooden notice-board on which was written in enormous letters: "To Be Sold," with remarks in smaller letters about the land and the name of the land agents. For the first time for years Owen Hood stood up in his place and left his fishing, and shouted questions across the river. The man answered with the greatest patience and good-humour; but it is probable that he went away convinced that he had been talking to a wandering lunatic.

That was the beginning of what was for Owen Hood a crawling nightmare. The change advanced slowly, by a process covering years, but it seemed to him all the time that he was helpless and paralysed in its presence, precisely as a man is paralysed in an actual nightmare. He laughed with an almost horrible laughter to think that a man in a modern society is supposed to be master of his fate and free to pursue his pleasures; when he has not power to prevent the daylight he looks on from being darkened, or the air he breathes from being turned to poison, or the silence that is his full possession from being shaken with the cacophony of hell. There was something, he thought grimly, in Dr Hunter's simple admiration for agricultural aristocracy. There was something in quite primitive and even barbarous aristocracy. Feudal lords went in fitfully for fights and forays; they put collars round the necks of some serfs; they occasionally put halters round the necks of a few of them. But they did not wage war day and night against the five senses of man.

There had appeared first on the river-bank small sheds and shanties, for workmen who seemed to be rather lengthily occupied in putting up larger sheds and shanties. To the very last, when the factory was finished, it was not easy for a traditional eye to distinguish between what was temporary and what was permanent. It did not look as if any of it could be permanent, if there were anything natural in the nature of things, so to speak. But whatever was the name and nature of that amorphous thing, it swelled and increased and even multiplied without clear division; until there stood on the river bank a great black patchwork block of buildings terminating in a tall brick factory chimney from which a stream of smoke mounted into the silent sky A heap of some sort of debris, scrapped iron and similar things, lay in the foreground; and a broken bar, red with rust, had fallen on the spot where the girl had been standing when she brought bluebells out of the wood.

He did not leave his island. Rural and romantic and sedentary as he may have seemed, he was not the son of an old revolutionist for nothing. It was not altogether in vain that his father had called him Robert Owen or that his friends had sometimes called him Robin Hood. Sometimes, indeed, his soul sank within him with a mortal sickness that was near to suicide, but more often he marched up and down in a militant fashion, being delighted to see the tall wild-flowers waving on the banks like flags within a stone's-throw of all he hated, and muttering, "Throw out the banners on the outward wall." He had already, when the estate of Marley Court was broken up for building, taken some steps to establish himself on the island, had built a sort of hut there, in which it was possible to picnic for considerable periods.

One morning when dawn was still radiant behind the dark factory and light lay in a satin sheen upon the water, there crept out upon that satin something like a thickening thread of a different colour and material. It was a thin ribbon of some other liquid that did not mingle with the water, but lay on top of it wavering like a worm; and Owen Hood watched it as a man watches a snake. It looked like a snake, having opalescent colours not without intrinsic beauty; but to him it was a very symbolic snake; like the serpent that destroyed Eden. A few days afterwards there were a score of snakes covering the surface; little crawling rivers that moved on the river but did not mix with it, being as alien as witch's oils. Later there came darker liquids with no pretensions to beauty, black and brown flakes of grease that floated heavily.

It was highly characteristic of Hood that to the last he was rather hazy about the nature and purpose of the factory; and therefore about the ingredients of the chemicals that were flowing into the river; beyond the fact that they were mostly of the oily sort and floated on the water in flakes and lumps, and that something resembling petrol seemed to predominate, used perhaps rather for power than raw material. He had heard a rustic rumour that the enterprise was devoted to hair-dye. It smelt rather like a soap factory. So far as he ever understood it, he gathered that it was devoted to what might be considered as a golden mean between hair-dye and soap, some kind of new and highly hygienic cosmetics. There had been a yet more feverish fashion in these things, since Professor Hake had written his book proving that cosmetics were of all things the most hygienic. And Hood had seen many of the meadows of his childhood now brightened and adorned by large notices inscribed "Why Grow Old?" with the portrait of a young woman grinning in a regrettable manner. The appropriate name on the notices was Bliss, and he gathered that it all had something to do with the great factory.

Resolved to know a little more than this about the matter, he began to make inquiries and complaints, and engaged in a correspondence which ended in an actual interview with some of the principal persons involved. The correspondence had gone on for a long time before it came anywhere near to anything so natural as that. Indeed, the correspondence for a long time was entirely on his side. For the big businesses are quite as unbusinesslike as the Government departments; they are no better in efficiency and much worse in manners. But he obtained his interview at last, and it was with a sense of sour amusement that he came face to face with four people whom he wanted to meet.

One was Sir Samuel Bliss, for he had not yet performed those party services which led to his being known to us all as Lord Normantowers. He was a small, alert man like a ferret, with bristles of grey beard and hair, and active or even agitated movements. The second was his manager, Mr Low, a stout, dark man with a thick nose and thick rings, who eyed strangers with a curious heavy suspicion like a congested sense of injury. It is believed that he expected to be persecuted. The third man was something of a surprise, for he was no other than his old friend Dr Horace Hunter, as healthy and hearty as ever, but even better dressed; as he now had a great official appointment as some kind of medical inspector of the sanitary conditions of the district. But the fourth man was the greatest surprise of all. For it appeared that their conference was honoured by so great a figure in the scientific world as Professor Hake himself, who had revolutionized the modern mind with his new discoveries about the complexion in relation to health. When Hood realized who he was, a light of somewhat sinister understanding dawned on his long face.

On this occasion the Professor advanced an even more interesting theory. He was a big, blond man with blinking eyes and a bull neck; and doubtless there was more in him than met the eye, as is the way with great men. He spoke last, and his theory was expounded with a certain air of finality. The manager had already stated that it was quite impossible for large quantities of petrol to have escaped, as only a given amount was used in the factory. Sir Samuel had explained, in what seemed an irascible and even irrelevant manner, that he had presented several parks to the public, and had the dormitories of his work-people decorated in the simplest and best taste, and nobody could accuse him of vandalism or not caring for beauty and all that. Then it was that Professor Hake explained the theory of the Protective Screen. Even if it were possible, he said, for some thin film of petrol to appear on the water, as it would not mix with the water the latter would actually be kept in a clearer condition. It would act, as it were, as a Cap; as does the gelatinous Cap upon certain preserved foods.

"That is a very interesting view," observed Hood; "I suppose you will write another book about that?"

"I think we are all the more privileged," remarked Bliss, "in hearing of the discovery in this personal fashion, before our expert has laid it before the public."

"Yes," said Hood, "your expert is very expert, isn't he – in writing books?"

Sir Samuel Bliss stiffened in all his bristles. "I trust," he said, "you are not implying any doubt that our expert is an expert."

"I have no doubt of your expert," answered Hood gravely, "I do not doubt either that he is expert or that he is yours."

"Really, gentlemen," cried Bliss in a sort of radiance of protest, "I think such an insinuation about a man in Professor Hake's position – "

"Not at all, not at all," said Hood soothingly, "I'm sure it's a most comfortable position."

The Professor blinked at him, but a light burned in the eyeballs under the heavy eyelids.

"If you come here talking like that – " he began, when Hood cut off his speech by speaking across him to somebody else, with a cheerful rudeness that was like a kick in its contempt.

"And what do you say, my dear doctor?" he observed, addressing Hunter. "You used to be almost as romantic as myself about the amenities of this place. Do you remember how much you admired the landlords for keeping the place quiet and select; and how you said the old families preserved the beauty of old England?"

There was a silence, and then the young doctor spoke.

"Well, it doesn't follow a fellow can't believe in progress. That's what's the matter with you, Hood; you don't believe in progress. We must move with the times; and somebody always has to suffer. Besides, it doesn't matter so much about river-water nowadays. It doesn't even matter so much about the main water-supply. When the new Bill is passed, people will be obliged to use the Bulton Filter in any case."

"I see," said Hood reflectively, "You first make a mess of the water for money, and then make a virtue of forcing people to clean it themselves."

"I don't know what you're talking about," said Hunter angrily.

"Well, I was thinking at the moment," said Hood in his rather cryptic way. "I was thinking about Mr Bulton. The man who owns the filters. I was wondering whether he might join us. We seem such a happy family party."

"I cannot see the use of prolonging this preposterous conversation," said Sir Samuel.

"Don't call the poor Professor's theory preposterous," remonstrated Hood. "A little fanciful, perhaps. And as for the doctor's view, surely there's nothing preposterous in that. You don't think the chemicals will poison all the fish I catch, do you, Doctor?"

"No, of course not," replied Hunter curtly

"They will adapt themselves by natural selection," said Hood dreamily. "They will develop organs suitable to an oily environment – will learn to love petrol."

"Oh, I have no time for this nonsense," said Hunter, and was turning to go, when Hood stepped in front of him and looked at him very steadily.

"You mustn't call natural selection nonsense," he said. "I know all about that, at any rate. I can't tell whether liquids tipped off the shore will fall into the river, because I don't understand hydraulics. I don't know whether your machinery makes a hell of a noise every morning, for I've never studied acoustics. I don't know whether it stinks or not, because I haven't read your expert's book on 'The Nose.' But I know all about adaptation to environment. I know that some of the lower organisms do really change with their changing conditions. I know there are creatures so low that they do survive by surrendering to every succession of mud and slime; and when things are slow they are slow, and when things are fast they are fast, and when things are filthy they are filthy I thank you for convincing me of that."

He did not wait for a reply, but walked out of the room after bowing curtly to the rest; and that was the end of the great conference on the question of riparian rights and perhaps the end of Thames Conservancy and of the old aristocratic England, with its good and ill.

The general public never heard very much about it; at least until one catastrophic scene which was to follow. There was some faint ripple of the question some months later, when Dr Horace Hunter was standing for Parliament in that division. One or two questions were asked about his duties in relation to river pollution; but it was soon apparent that no party particularly wished to force the issue against the best opinions advanced on the other side. The greatest living authority on hygiene, Professor Hake, had actually written to *The Times* (in the interests of science) to say that in such a hypothetical case as that mentioned, a medical man could only do what Dr Hunter had apparently done. It so happened that the chief captain of industry in that part of the Thames Valley, Sir Samuel Bliss, had himself, after gravely weighing the rival policies, decided to Vote for Hunter. The great organizer's own mind was detached and philosophical in the matter; but it seems that his manager, a Mr Low, was of the same politics and a more practical and pushful spirit; warmly urging the claims of Hunter on his work-people; pointing out the many practical advantages they would gain by voting for that physician, and the still more practical disadvantages they might suffer by not doing so. Hence it followed that the blue ribbons, which were the local badges of the Hunterians, were not only to be found attached to the iron railings and wooden posts of the factory, but to various human figures, known as "hands," which moved to and fro in it.

Hood took no interest in the election; but while it was proceeding he followed the matter a little further in another form. He was a lawyer, a lazy, but in some ways a learned one; for, his tastes being studious, he had originally learned the trade he had never used. More in defiance than in hope, he once carried the matter into the Courts, pleading his own cause on the basis of a law of Henry the Third against frightening the fish of the King's liege subjects in the Thames Valley. The judge, in giving judgment, complimented him on the ability and plausibility of his contention, but ultimately rejected it on grounds equally historic and remote. His lordship argued that no test seemed to be provided for ascertaining the degree of fear in the fish, or whether it amounted to that bodily fear of which the law took cognizance. But the learned judge pointed out the precedent of a law of Richard the Second against certain witches who had frightened children; which had been interpreted by so great an authority as Coke in the sense that the child "must return and of his own will testify to his fear." It did not seem to be alleged that any one of the fish in question had returned and laid any such testimony before any proper authority; and he therefore gave judgment for the defendants. And when the learned judge happened to meet Lord Normantowers (as he was by this time) out at dinner that evening, he was gaily rallied and congratulated by that new nobleman on the lucidity and finality of his judgment. Indeed, the learned judge had really relished the logic both of his own and Hood's contention; but the conclusion was what he would have come to in any case. For our judges are not hampered by any hidebound code; they are progressive, like Dr Hunter, and ally themselves on principle with the progressive forces of the age, especially those they are likely to meet out at dinner.

But it was this abortive law case that led up to something that altogether obliterated it in a blaze of glory so far as Mr Owen Hood was concerned. He had just left the courts, and turning down the streets that led in the direction of the station, he made his way thither in something of a brown study, as was his wont. The streets were filled with faces; it struck him for the first time that there were thousands and thousands of people in the world. There were more faces at the railway station, and then, when he had glanced idly at four or five of them, he saw one that was to him as incredible as the face of the dead.

She was coming casually out of the tea-room, carrying a handbag, just like anybody else. That mystical perversity of his mind, which had insisted on sealing up the sacred memory like something hardly to be sought in mere curiosity, had fixed it in its original colours and setting, like something of which no detail could be changed without the vision dissolving. He would have conceived it almost impossible that she could appear in anything but white or out of anything but a wood. And he found himself turned topsy-turvy by an old and common incredulity of men in his condition; being startled by the coincidence that blue suited her as well as white; and that in what he remembered of that woodland there was something else; something to be said even for teashops and railway stations.

She stopped in front of him and her pale, fluttering eyelids lifted from her blue-grey eyes.

"Why" she said, "you are the boy that jumped in the river!"

"I'm no longer a boy," answered Hood, "but I'm ready to jump in the river again."

"Well, don't jump on the railway-line," she said, as he turned with a swiftness suggestive of something of the kind.

"To tell you the truth," he said, "I was thinking of jumping into a railway-train. Do you mind if I jump into your railway-train?"

"Well, I'm going to Birkstead," she said rather doubtfully.

Mr Owen Hood did not in the least care where she was going, as he had resolved to go there; but as a matter of fact, he remembered a wayside station on that line that lay very near to what he had in view; so he tumbled into the carriage if possible with more alacrity; and landscapes shot by them as they sat looking in a dazed and almost foolish fashion at each other. At last the girl smiled with a sense of the absurdity of the thing.

"I heard about you from a friend of yours," she said; "he came to call on us soon after it happened; at least that was when he first came. You know Dr Hunter, don't you?"

"Yes," replied Owen, a shadow coming over his shining hour. "Do you – do you know him well?"

"I know him pretty well now," said Miss Elizabeth Seymour.

The shadow on his spirit blackened swiftly; he suspected something quite suddenly and savagely. Hunter, in Crane's old phrase, was not a man who let the grass grow under his feet. It was so like him to have somehow used the incident as an introduction to the Seymours. Things were always stepping-stones for Hunter, and the little rock in the river had been a stepping-stone to the country-house. But was the country-house a stepping-stone to something else? Suddenly Hood realized that all his angers had been very abstract angers. He had never hated a man before.

At that moment the train stopped at the station of Cowford.

"I wish you'd get out here with me," he said abruptly, "only for a little – and it might be the last time. I want you to do something."

She looked at him with a curious expression and said in a rather low voice, "What do you want me to do?"

"I want you to come and pick bluebells," he said harshly.

She stepped out of the train, and they went up a winding country road without a word.

"I remember!" she said suddenly. "When you get to the top of this hill you see the wood where the bluebells were, and your little island beyond."

"Come on and see it," said Owen.

They stepped on the crest of the hill and stood. Below them the black factory belched its livid smoke into the air; and where the wood had been were rows of little houses like boxes, built of dirty yellow brick.

Hood spoke. "And when you shall see the abomination of desolation sitting in the Holy of Holies – isn't that when the world is supposed to end? I wish the world would end now; with you and me standing on a hill."

She was staring at the place with parted lips and more than her ordinary pallor; he knew she understood something monstrous and symbolic in the scene; yet her first remark was jerky and trivial. On the nearest of the yellow brick boxes were visible the cheap colours of various advertisements; and larger than the rest a blue poster proclaiming "Vote for Hunter." With a final touch of bathos, Hood remembered that it was the last and most sensational day of the election. But the girl had already found her voice.

"Is that Dr Hunter?" she asked with commonplace curiosity; "is he standing for Parliament?"

A load that lay on Hood's mind like a rock suddenly rose like an eagle; and he felt as if the hill he stood on were higher than Everest. By the insight of his own insanity, he knew well enough that *she* would have known well enough whether Hunter was standing, if – if there had been anything like what he supposed. The removal of the steadying weight staggered him, and he had said something quite indefensible.

"I thought you would know. I thought you and he were probably – well, the truth is I thought you were engaged, though I really don't know why."

"I can't imagine why," said Elizabeth Seymour. "I heard he was engaged to Lord Normantower's daughter. They've got our old place now, you know."

There was a silence and then Hood spoke suddenly in a loud and cheerful voice.

"Well, what I say is, 'Vote for Hunter,'" he said heartily. "After all, why not vote for Hunter? Good old Hunter! I hope he'll be a Member of Parliament. I hope he'll be Prime Minister. I hope he'll be President of the World State that Wells talks about. By George, he deserves to be Emperor of the Solar System."

"But why," she protested, "why should he deserve all that?"

"For not being engaged to you, of course," he replied.

"Oh!" she said, and something of a secret shiver in her voice went through him like a silver bell.

Abruptly, all of a sudden, the rage of raillery seemed to leave his voice and his face, so that his Napoleonic profile looked earnest and eager and much younger, like the profile of the young Napoleon. His wide shoulders lost the slight stoop that books had given them, and his rather wild red hair fell away from his lifted head.

"There is one thing I must tell you about him," he said, "and one thing you must hear about me. My friends tell me I am a drifter and a dreamer; that I let the grass grow under my feet; I must tell you at least how and why I once let it grow. Three days after that day by the river, I talked to Hunter; he was attending me and he talked about it and you. Of course he knew nothing about either. But he is a practical man; a very practical man; he does not dream or drift. From the way he talked I knew he was considering even then how the accident could be turned to account; to his account and perhaps to mine too; for he is good-natured; yes, he is quite good-natured. I think that if I had taken his hint and formed a sort of social partnership, I might have known you six years sooner, not as a memory, but – an acquaintance. And I could not do it. Judge me how you will, I could not bring myself to do it. That is what is meant by being born with a bee in the bonnet, with an impediment in the speech, with a stumbling-block in the path, with a sulky scruple in the soul. I could not bear to approach you by that door, with that gross and grinning flunkey holding it open. I could not bear that suffocatingly substantial snob to bulk so big in my story or know so much of my secret. A revulsion I could never utter made me feel that the vision should remain my own even by remaining unfulfilled; but it should not be vulgarized. That is what is meant by being a failure in life. And when my best friend made a prophecy about me, and said there was something I should never do, I thought he was right."

"Why what do you mean?" she asked rather faintly, "what was it you would never do?"

"Never mind that now," he said, with the shadow of a returning smile. "Rather strange things are stirring in me just now, and who knows but I may attempt something yet? But before all else, I must make clear for once what I am and for what I lived. There are men like me in the world; I am far from thinking they are the best or the most valuable; but they exist, to confound all the clever people and the realists and the new novelists. There has been and there is only one thing for me; something that in the normal sense I never even knew. I walked about the world blind, with my eyes turned inwards, looking at you. For days after a night when I had dreamed of you, I was broken; like a man who had seen a ghost. I read over and over the great and grave lines of the old poets, because they alone were worthy of you. And when I saw you again by chance, I thought the world had already ended; and it was that return and tryst beyond the grave that is too good to be true."

"I do not think," said answered in a low voice, "that the belief is too good to be true."

As he looked at her a thrill went through him like a message too swift to be understood; and at the back of his mind something awoke that repeated again and again like a song the same words: "too good to be true." There was always something pathetic, even in her days of pride, about the short-sighted look of her half-closed eyes; but it was for other reasons that they were now blinking in the strong white sunlight, almost as if they were blind. They were blind and bright with tears: she mastered her voice and it was steady.

"You talk about failures," she said. "I suppose most people would call me a failure and all my people failures now; except those who would say we never failed, because we never had to try. Anyhow, we're all poor enough now; I don't know whether you know that I'm teaching music. I dare say we deserved to go. I dare say we were useless. Some of us tried to be harmless. But – but now I *must* say something, about some of us who tried rather hard to be harmless – in that way. The new people will tell you those ideals were Victorian and Tennysonian, and all the rest of it – well, it doesn't matter what they say. They know quite as little about us as we about them. But to you, when you talk like that...what can I do, but tell you that if we were stiff, if we were cold, if we were careful and conservative, it was because deep down in our souls some of us *did* believe that there might be loyalty and love like that, for which a woman might well wait even to the end of the world. What is it to these people if we chose not to be drugged or distracted with anything less worthy? But it would be hard indeed if when I find it *does* exist after all...hard on you, harder on me, if when I had really found it at last..." The catch in her voice came again and silence caught and held her.

He took one stride forward as into the heart of a whirlwind; and they met on the top of that windy hill as if they had come from the ends of the earth.

"This is an epic," he said, "which is rather an action than a word. I have lived with words too long."

"What do you mean?"

"I mean you have turned me into a man of action," he replied. "So long as you were in the past, nothing was better than the past. So long as you were only a dream, nothing was better than dreaming. But now I am going to do something that no man has ever done before."

He turned towards the valley and flung out his hand with a gesture, almost as if the hand had held a sword.

"I am going to break the Prophecy," he cried in a loud voice. "I am going to defy the omens of my doom and make fun of my evil star. Those who called me a failure shall own I have succeeded where all humanity has failed. The real hero is not he who is bold enough to fulfil the predictions, but he who is bold enough to falsify them. And you shall see one falsified tonight."

"What in the world are you going to do?" she asked.

He laughed suddenly "The first thing to do," he cried, swinging round with a new air of resolution and even cheerfulness, "the very first thing to do is to Vote For Hunter. Or, at any rate, help to get him into Parliament."

"But why in the world," she asked wondering, "should you want so much to get Dr Hunter into Parliament?"

"Well, one must do something," he said with an appearance of easy good sense, "to celebrate the occasion. We must do something; and after all he must go somewhere, poor devil. You will say why not throw him into the river? It would relieve the feelings and make a splash. But I'm going to make something much bigger than a splash. Besides, I don't want him in my nice river. I'd much rather pick him up and throw him all the way to Westminster. Much more sensible and suitable. Obviously there ought to be a brass band and a torchlight procession somewhere tonight; and why shouldn't he have a bit of the fun?"

He stopped suddenly as if surprised at his own words; for indeed his own phrase had fallen, for him, with the significance of a falling star.

"Of course!" he muttered. "A torchlight procession! I've been feeling that what I wanted was trumpets and what I really want is torches. Yes, I believe it could be done! Yes, the hour is come! By stars and blazes, I will give him a torchlight procession!"

He had been almost dancing with excitement on the top of the ridge; now he suddenly went bounding down the slope beyond, calling to the girl to follow, as carelessly as if they had been two children playing at hide and seek. Strangely enough, perhaps, she did follow; more strangely still when we consider the extravagant scenes through which she allowed herself to be led. They were scenes more insanely incongruous with all her sensitive and even secretive dignity than if she had been changing hats with a costermonger on a Bank Holiday. For there the world would only be loud with vulgarity, and here it was also loud with lies. She could never have described that Saturnalia of a political election; but she did dimly feel the double impression of a harlequinade at the end of a pantomime and of Hood's phrase about the end of the world. It was as if a Bank Holiday could also be a Day of Judgment. But as the farce could no longer offend her, so the tragedy could no longer terrify. She went through it all with a wan smile, which perhaps nobody in the world would have known her well enough to interpret. It was not in the normal sense excitement; yet it was something much more positive than patience. In a sense perhaps, more than ever before in her lonely life, she was walled up in her ivory tower; but it was all alight within, as if it were lit with candles or lined with gold.

Hood's impetuous movements brought them to the bank of the river and the outer offices of the factory, all of which were covered with the coloured posters of the candidature, and one of which was obviously fitted up as a busy and bustling committee-room. Hood actually met Mr Low coming out of it, buttoned up in a fur coat and bursting with speechless efficiency. But Mr Low's beady black eyes glistened with an astonishment bordering on suspicion when Hood in the most hearty fashion offered his sympathy and co-operation. That strange subconscious fear, that underlay all the wealthy manager's success and security in this country, always came to the surface at the sight of Owen Hood's long ironical face. Just at that moment, however, one of the local agents rushed at him in a distracted fashion, with telegrams in his hand. They were short of canvassers; they were short of cars; they were short of speakers; the crowd at Little Puddleton had been waiting half an hour; Dr Hunter could not get round to them till ten past nine, and so on. The agent in his agony would probably have hailed a Margate nigger and entrusted him with the cause of the great National Party, without any really philosophical inquiry into the nigger's theory of citizenship. For all such over-practical push and bustle in our time is always utterly unpractical at the last minute and in the long run. On that night Robert Owen Hood would have been encouraged to go anywhere and say anything; and he did. It might be interesting to imagine what the lady thought about it; but it is possible that she did not think about it. She had a radiantly abstracted sense of passing through a number of ugly rooms and sheds with flaring gas and stacks of leaflets behind which little irritable men ran about like rabbits. The walls were covered with large allegorical pictures printed in line or in a few bright colours, representing Dr Hunter as clad in armour, as slaying dragons, as rescuing ladies rather like classical goddesses, and so on. Lest it should be too literally understood that Dr Hunter was in the habit of killing dragons in his daily round, as a form of field-sport, the dragon was inscribed with its name in large letters. Apparently its name was "National Extravagance." Lest there should be any doubt about the alternative which Dr Hunter had discovered as a corrective to extravagance, the sword which he was thrusting through the dragon's body was inscribed with the word "Economy." Elizabeth Seymour, through whose happy but bewildered mind these pictures passed, could not but reflect vaguely that she herself had lately had to practise a good deal of economy and resist a good many temptations to extravagance; but it would never have occurred to her unaided imagination to conceive the action as that of plunging a sword into a scaly monster of immense size. In the central committee-room they actually came face to face for a moment with the candidate, who came in very hot and breathless with a silk hat on the back of his head; where he had possibly forgotten it, for he certainly did not remove it. She was a little ashamed of being sensitive about such trifles; but she came to the conclusion that she would not like to have a husband standing for Parliament.

"We've rounded up all those people down Bleak Row," said Dr Hunter. "No good going down The Hole and those filthy places. No vote there. Streets ought to be abolished and the people too."

"Well, we've had a very good meeting in the Masonic Hall," said the agent cheerfully. "Lord Normantowers spoke, and really he got through all right. Told some stories, you know; and they stood it capitally"

"And now," said Owen Hood, slapping his hands together in an almost convivial manner, "what about this torchlight procession?"

"This what procession?" asked the agent.

"Do you mean to tell me," said Hood sternly, "that arrangements are not complete for the torchlight procession of Dr Hunter? That you are going to let this night of triumph pass without kindling a hundred flames to light the path of the conqueror? Do you realize that the hearts of a whole people have spontaneously stirred and chosen him? That the suffering poor murmured in their sleep 'Vote for Hunter' long before the Caucus came by a providential coincidence to the same conclusion? Would not the people in The Hole set fire to their last poor sticks of furniture to do him honour? Why from this chair alone – "

He caught up the chair on which Hunter had been sitting and began to break it enthusiastically. In this he was hastily checked; but he actually succeeded in carrying the company with him in his proposal, thus urged at the eleventh hour.

By nightfall he had actually organized his torchlight procession, escorting the triumphant Hunter, covered with blue ribbons, to the riverside, rather as if the worthy doctor were to be baptized like a convert or drowned like a witch. For that matter, Hood might possibly intend to burn the witch; for he brandished the blazing torch he carried so as to make a sort of halo round Hunter's astonished countenance. Then, springing on the scrap-heap by the brink of the river, he addressed the crowd for the last time.

"Fellow-citizens, we meet upon the shore of the Thames, the Thames which is to Englishmen all that the Tiber ever was to Romans. We meet in a valley which has been almost as much the haunt of English poets as of English birds. Never was there an art so native to our island as our old national tradition of landscape-painting in water-colour; never was that water-colour so luminous or so delicate as when dedicated to these holy waters. It was in such a scene that one of the most exquisite of our elder poets repeated as a burden to his meditations the single line, 'Sweet Thames, run softly till I end my song.'

"Rumours have been heard of some intention to trouble these waters; but we have been amply reassured. Names that now stand as high as those of our national poets and painters are a warrant that the stream is still as clear and pure and beneficent as of old. We all know the beautiful work that Mr Bulton has done in the matter of filters. Dr Hunter supports Mr Bulton. I mean Mr Bulton supports Dr Hunter. I may also mention no less a man than Mr Low. Sweet Thames, run softly till I end my song.

"But then, for that matter, we all support Dr Hunter. I myself have always found him quite supportable; I should say quite satisfactory He is truly a progressive, and nothing gives me greater pleasure than to watch him progress. As somebody said, I lie awake at night; and in the silence of the whole universe, I seem to hear him climbing, climbing, climbing. All the numerous patients among whom he has laboured so successfully in this locality will join in a heartfelt expression of joy if he passes to the higher world of Westminster. I trust I shall not be misunderstood. Sweet Thames, run softly till I end my song.

"My only purpose tonight is to express that unanimity. There may have been times when I differed from Dr Hunter; but I am glad to say that all that is passed, and I have now nothing but the most friendly feelings towards him, for reasons which I will not mention, though I have plenty to say. In token of this reconciliation I here solemnly cast from me this torch. As that firebrand is quenched in the cool crystal waters of that sacred stream, so shall all such feuds perish in the heating pool of universal peace."

Before anybody knew what he was doing, he had whirled his flambeau in a flaming wheel round his head and sent it flying like a meteor out into the dim eddies of the river.

The next moment a short, sharp cry was uttered, and every face in that crowd was staring at the river. All the faces were visibly staring, for they were all lit up as by a ghastly firelight by a wide wan unnatural flame that leapt up from the very surface of the stream; a flame that the crowd watched as it might have watched a comet.

"There," cried Owen Hood, turning suddenly on the girl and seizing her arm, as if demanding congratulations. "So much for old Crane's prophecy!"

"Who in the world is Old Crane?" she asked, "and what did he prophesy? Is he something like Old Moore?"

"Only an old friend," said Hood hastily, "only an old friend of mine. It's what he said that's so important. He didn't like my moping about with books and a fishing-rod, and he said, standing on that very island, 'You may know a lot; but I don't think you'll ever set the Thames on fire. I'll eat my hat if you do.' "

But the story of how Old Crane ate his hat is one upon which some readers at least can look back as on labour and suffering bravely endured. And if it be possible for any of them to desire to know any more either about Mr Crane or Mr Hood, then they must gird themselves for the ordeal of reading the story of The Unobtrusive Traffic of Captain Pierce, and their trials are for a time deferred.

III

The Unobtrusive Traffic of Captain Pierce

Those acquainted with Colonel Crane and Mr Owen Hood, the lawyer, may or may not be concerned to know that they partook of an early lunch of eggs and bacon and beer at the inn called the Blue Boar, which stands at the turn of a steep road scaling a wooded ridge in the West Country. Those unacquainted with them may be content to know that the Colonel was a sunburnt, neatly-dressed gentleman, who looked taciturn and was; while the lawyer was a more rusty red-haired gentleman with a long Napoleonic face, who looked taciturn and was rather talkative. Crane was fond of good cooking; and the cooking in that secluded inn was better than that of a Soho restaurant and immeasurably better than that of a fashionable restaurant. Hood was fond of the legends and less-known aspects of the English countryside; and that valley had a quality of repose with a stir of refreshment, as if the west wind had been snared in it and tamed into a summer air. Both had a healthy admiration for beauty, in ladies as well as landscapes; although (or more probably because) both were quite romantically attached to the wives they had married under rather romantic circumstances, which are related elsewhere for such as can wrestle with so steep a narrative. And the girl who waited on them, the daughter of the innkeeper, was herself a very agreeable thing to look at; she was of a slim and quiet sort with a head that moved like a brown bird, brightly and as it were unexpectedly. Her manners were full of unconscious dignity, for her father, old John Hardy, was the type of old innkeeper who had the status, if not of a gentleman, at least of a yeoman. He was not without education and ability; a grizzled man with a keen, stubborn face that might have belonged to Cobbett, whose *Register* he still read on winters' nights. Hardy was well known to Hood, who had the same sort of antiquarian taste in revolutions.

There was little sound in the valley or the brilliant void of sky; the notes of birds fell only intermittently; a faint sound of tapping came from the hills opposite where the wooded slope was broken here and there by the bare face of a quarry, and a distant aeroplane passed and repassed, leaving a trail of faint thunder. The two men at lunch took no more notice of it than if it had been a buzzing fly; but an attentive study of the girl might have suggested that she was at least conscious of the fly. Occasionally she looked at it, when no one was looking at her; for the rest, she had rather a marked appearance of not looking at it.

"Good bacon you get here," remarked Colonel Crane.

"The best in England, and in the matter of breakfast England is the Earthly Paradise," replied Hood readily. "I can't think why we should descend to boast of the British Empire when we have bacon and eggs to boast of. They ought to be quartered on the Royal Arms: three pigs passant and three poached eggs on a chevron. It was bacon and eggs that gave all that morning glory to the English poets; it must have been a man who had a breakfast like this who could rise with that giant gesture: 'Night's candles are burnt out; and jocund day – ' "

"Bacon did write Shakespeare, in fact," said the Colonel.

"This sort of bacon did," answered the other laughing; then, noticing the girl within earshot, he added: "We are saying how good your bacon is, Miss Hardy."

"It is supposed to be very good," she said with legitimate pride, "but I am afraid you won't get much more of it. People aren't going to be allowed to keep pigs much longer."

"Not allowed to keep pigs!" ejaculated the Colonel in astonishment.

"By the old regulations they had to be away from the house, and we've got ground enough for that, though most of the cottagers hadn't. But now they say the law is evaded, and the county council are going to stop pig-keeping altogether."

"Silly swine," snorted the Colonel.

"The epithet is ill chosen," replied Hood. "Men are lower than swine when they do not appreciate swine. But really I don't know what the world's coming to. What will the next generation be like without proper pork? And, talking about the next generation, what has become of your young friend Pierce? He said he was coming down, but he can't have come by that train."

"I think Captain Pierce is up there, sir," said Joan Hardy in a correct voice, as she unobtrusively withdrew.

Her tone might have indicated that the gentleman was upstairs, but her momentary glance had been towards the blue emptiness of the sky. Long after she was gone, Owen Hood remained staring up into it, until he saw the aeroplane darting and wheeling like a swallow.

"Is that Hilary Pierce up there?" he inquired, "looping the loop and playing the lunatic generally. What the devil is he doing?"

"Showing off," said the Colonel shortly and drained his pewter mug.

"But why should he show off to us?" asked Hood.

"He jolly well wouldn't," replied the Colonel. "Showing off to the girl, of course." Then after a pause he added: "A very nice girl."

"A very good girl," said Owen Hood gravely. "If there's anything going on, you may be sure it's all straight and serious."

The Colonel blinked a little. "Well, times change," he said. "I suppose I'm old-fashioned myself; but speaking as an old Tory, I must confess he might do worse."

"Yes," replied Hood, "and speaking as an old Radical, I should say he could hardly do better."

While they were speaking the erratic aviator had eventually swept earthwards towards a flat field at the foot of the slope, and was now coming towards them. Hilary Pierce had rather the look of a poet than a professional aviator; and though he had distinguished himself in the war, he was very probably one of those whose natural dream was rather of conquering the air than conquering the enemy. His yellow hair was longer and more untidy than when he was in the army; and there was a touch of something irresponsible in his roving blue eye. He had a vein of pugnacity in him, however, as was soon apparent. He had paused to speak to Joan Hardy by the rather tumbledown pig-sty in the corner, and when he came towards the breakfast table he seemed transfigured as with flame.

"What's all this infernal insane foolery?" he demanded. "Who has the damned impudence to tell the Hardys they mustn't keep pigs? Look here, the time is come when we must burst up all this sort of thing. I'm going to do something desperate."

"You've been doing desperate things enough for this morning," said Hood. "I advise you to take a little desperate luncheon. Do sit down, there's a good fellow, and don't stamp about like that."

"No, but look here – "

Pierce was interrupted by Joan Hardy, who appeared quietly at his elbow and said demurely to the company: "There's a gentleman here who asks if he may be pardoned for speaking to you."

The gentleman in question stood some little way behind in a posture that was polite but so stiff and motionless as almost to affect the nerves. He was clad in so complete and correct a version of English light holiday attire that they felt quite certain he was a foreigner. But their imaginations ranged the Continent in vain in the attempt to imagine what sort of foreigner. By the immobility of his almost moonlike face, with its faintly bilious tinge, he might almost have been a Chinaman. But when he spoke, they could instantly locate the alien accent.

"Very much distressed to butt in, gentlemen," he said, "but this young lady allows you are first-class academic authorities on the sights of this locality. I've been mouching around trying to hit the trail of an antiquity or two, but I don't seem to know the way to pick it up. If you'd be so kind as to put me wise about the principal architectural styles and historic items of this region, I'd be under a great obligation."

As they were a little slow in recovering from their first surprise, he added patiently:

"My name is Enoch B Oates, and I'm pretty well known in Michigan, but I've bought a little place near here; I've looked about this little planet and I've come to think the safest and brightest place for a man with a few dollars is the place of a squire in your fine old feudal landscape. So the sooner I'm introduced to the more mellow medieval buildings the better."

In Hilary Pierce the astonishment had given place to an ardour bordering on ecstasy.

"Mediaeval buildings! Architectural styles!" he cried enthusiastically "You've come to the right shop, Mr Oates. I'll show you an ancient building, a sacred building, in an architectural style of such sublime antiquity that you'll want to cart it all away to Michigan, as they tried to do with Glastonbury Abbey. You shall be privileged to see one historic institution before you die or before all history is forgotten."

He was walking towards the corner of the little kitchen garden attached to the inn, waving his arm with wild gestures of encouragement; and the American was following him with the same stiff politeness, looking weirdly like an automaton.

"Look on our architectural style before it perishes," cried Pierce dramatically, pointing to the pig-sty, which looked rather a ramshackle affair of leaning and broken boards hung loosely together, though in practice it was practical enough. "This, the most unmistakably mellow of all medieval buildings, may soon be only a memory But when this edifice falls England will fall, and the world will shake with the shock of doom."

The American had what he himself might have described as a poker face; it was impossible to discover whether his utterances indicated the extreme of innocence or of irony.

"And would you say," he asked, "that this monument exemplifies the medieval or Gothic architectural school?"

"I should hardly call it strictly Perpendicular," answered Pierce, "but there is no doubt that it is Early English."

"You would say it is antique, anyhow?" observed Mr Oates.

"I have every reason to believe," affirmed Pierce solemnly, "that Gurth the Swineherd made use of this identical building. I have no doubt that it is in fact far older. The best authorities believe that the Prodigal Son stayed here for some time, and the pigs – those noble and much maligned animals – gave him such excellent advice that he returned to his family. And now, Mr Oates, they say that all that magnificent heritage is to be swept away. But it shall not be. We shall not so easily submit to all the vandals and vulgar tyrants who would thus tear down our temples and our holy places. The pig-sty shall rise again in a magnificent resurrection – larger pig-stys, loftier pig-stys, shall yet cover the land; the towers and domes and spires of statelier and more ideal pig-stys, in the most striking architectural styles, shall again declare the victory of the holy hog over his unholy oppressors."

"And meanwhile," said Colonel Crane dryly, "I think Mr Oates had much better begin with the church down by the river. Very fine Norman foundations and traces of the Roman brick. The vicar understands his church, too, and would give Mr Oates rather more reliable information than you do."

A little while later, when Mr Oates had passed on his way, the Colonel curtly reproved his young friend.

"Bad form," he said, "making fun of a foreigner asking for information."

But Pierce turned on him with the same heat on his face.

"But I wasn't making fun. I was quite serious."

They stared at him steadily and he laughed slightly but went on with undiminished fire.

"Symbolical perhaps but serious," he said. "I may seem to have been talking a bit wildly, but let me tell you the time has come to be wild. We've all been a lot too tame. I do mean, as much as I ever meant anything, to fight for the resurrection and the return of the pig; and he shall yet return as a wild boar that will rend the hunters."

He looked up and his eye caught the blue heraldic shape on the sign-board of the inn.

"And there is our wooden ensign!" he cried, pointing in the same dramatic fashion. "We will go into battle under the banner of the Blue Boar."

"Loud and prolonged cheers," said Crane politely, "and now come away and don't spoil the peroration. Owen wants to potter about the local antiquities, like Mr Oates. I'm more interested in novelties. Want to look at that machine of yours."

They began to descend the zig-zag pebbled path fenced and embanked with hedges and flower-beds like a garden grown on a staircase, and at every corner Hood had to remonstrate with the loitering youth.

"Don't be for ever gazing back on the paradise of pigs," he said, "or you'll be turned into a pillar of salt, or possibly of mustard as more appropriate to such meat. They won't run away yet. There are other creatures formed by the Creator for the contemplation of man; there are other things made by man after the pattern of the creatures, from the great White Horses of Wessex to that great white bird on which you yourself flew among the birds. Fine subject for a poem of the first and last things."

"Bird that lays rather dreadful eggs," said Crane. "In the next war – Why, where the deuce has he gone?"

"Pigs, pigs," said Hood sadly. "The overpowering charm which pigs exercise upon us at a certain time of life; when we hear their trotters in our dreams and their little curly tails twine about us like the tendrils of the vine – "

"Oh, bosh," said the Colonel.

For indeed Mr Hilary Pierce had vanished in a somewhat startling manner, ducking under the corner of a hedge and darting up a steeper path, over a gate and across the corner of a hayfield, where a final bound through bursting bushes brought him on top of a low wall looking down at the pig-sty and Miss Joan Hardy, who was calmly walking away from it. He sprang down on to the path; the morning sun picked out everything in clear colours like a child's toy-book; and standing with his hands spread out and his wisps of yellow hair brushed in all directions by the bushes, he recalled an undignified memory of Shock-Headed Peter.

"I felt I must speak to you before I went," he said. "I'm going away, not exactly on active service, but on business – on very active business. I feel like the fellows did when they went to the war…and what they wanted to do first.... I am aware that a proposal over a pig-sty is not so symbolical to some as to me, but really and truly… I don't know whether I mentioned it, but you may be aware that I worship you."

Joan Hardy was quite aware of it; but the conventionalities in her case were like concentric castle walls; the world-old conventions of the countryside. There was in them the stiff beauty of old country dances and the slow and delicate needlework of a peasantry. Of all the ladies whose figures must be faintly traced in the tapestry of these frivolous tales of chivalry, the most reticent and dignified was the one who was not in the worldly sense a lady at all.

She stood looking at him in silence, and he at her; as the lift of her head had some general suggestion of a bird, the line of her profile had a delicate suggestion of a falcon, and her face was of the fine tint that has no name, unless we could talk of a bright brown.

"Really, you seem in a terrible hurry," she said. "I don't want to be talked to in a rush like this."

"I apologize," he said. "I can't help being in a rush, but I didn't want you to be in a rush. I only wanted you to know. I haven't done anything to deserve you, but I am going to try. I'm going off to work; I feel sure you believe in quiet steady work for a young man."

"Are you going into the bank?" she asked innocently. "You said your uncle was in a bank."

"I hope all my conversation was not on that level," he replied. And indeed he would have been surprised if he had known how exactly she remembered all such dull details he had ever mentioned about himself; and how little she knew in comparison about his theories and fancies, which he thought so much more important.

"Well," he said with engaging frankness, "it would be an exaggeration to say I am going into a bank; though of course there are banks and banks. Why, I know a bank whereupon the wild thyme – I beg your pardon, I mean I know a lot of more rural and romantic occupations that are really quite as safe as the bank. The truth is, I think of going into the bacon trade. I think I see an opening for a brisk young man in the ham and pork business. When you see me next I shall be travelling in pork; an impenetrable disguise."

"You mustn't come here, then," she answered. "It won't be allowed here by that time. The neighbours would – "

"Fear not," he said, "I should be a commercial traveller. Oh, such a very commercial traveller. As for not coming here, the thing seems quite unthinkable. You must at least let me write to you every hour or so. You must let me send you a few presents every morning."

"I'm sure my father wouldn't like you to send me presents," she said gravely.

"Ask your father to wait," said Pierce earnestly. "Ask him to wait till he's seen the presents. You see, mine will be rather curious presents. I don't think he'll disapprove of them. I think he'll approve of them. I think he'll congratulate me on my simple tastes and sound business principles. The truth is, dear Joan, I've committed myself to a rather important enterprise. You needn't be frightened; I promise I won't trouble you again till it succeeds. I will be content that you know it is for you I do it; and shall continue to do it, if I defy the world." He sprang up on the wall again and stood there staring down at her almost indignantly.

"That anybody should forbid *you* to keep pigs," he cried. "That anybody should forbid you to do anything. That anybody should dispute *your* right to keep pet crocodiles if you like! That is the unpardonable sin; that is the supreme blasphemy and crime against the nature of things, which shall not go unavenged. You shall have pigs, I say, if the skies fall and the whole world is whelmed in war."

He disappeared like a flash behind the high bank and the wall, and Joan went back in silence to the inn.

The first incident of the war did not seem superficially encouraging, though the hero of it seemed by no means discouraged by it. As reported in the police news of various papers, Hilary Patrick Pierce, formerly of the Flying Corps, was arrested for driving pigs into the county of Bluntshire, in contravention of the regulations made for the public health. He seemed to have had almost as much trouble with the pigs as with the police; but he made a witty and eloquent speech on being arrested, to which the police and the pigs appeared to be equally unresponsive. The incident was considered trivial and his punishment was trifling; but the occasion was valued by some of the authorities as giving an opportunity for the final elucidation and establishment of the new rule.

For this purpose it was fortunate that the principal magistrate of the bench was no less a person than the celebrated hygienist, Sir Horace Hunter, OBE MD, who had begun life, as some may remember, as a successful suburban doctor and had likewise distinguished himself as an officer of health in the Thames Valley. To him indeed had been largely due the logical extension of the existing precautions against infection from the pig; though he was fully supported by his fellow magistrates, one being Mr Rosenbaum Low, millionaire and formerly manager of Bliss and Co., and the other the young Socialist, Mr Amyas Minns, famous for his exposition of Shaw on the Simple Life, who sat on the bench as a Labour alderman. All concurred in the argument of Sir Horace, that just as all the difficulties and doubtful cases raised by the practice of moderate drinking had been simplified by the solution of Prohibition, so the various quarrels and evasions about swine-fever were best met by a straightforward and simple regulation against swine. In the very improper remarks which he offered after the trial, the prisoner appears to have said that as his three judges were a Jew, a vegetarian, and a quack doctor on the make, he was not surprised that they did not appreciate pork.

The next luncheon at which the three friends met was in a sufficiently different setting; for the Colonel had invited the other two to his club in London. It would have been almost impossible to have been that sort of Colonel without having that sort of club. But as a matter of fact, he very seldom went there. On this occasion it was Owen Hood who arrived first and was by instructions escorted by a waiter to a table in a bow window overlooking the Green Park. Knowing Crane's military punctuality, Hood fancied that he might have mistaken the time; and while looking for the note of invitation in his pocket-book, he paused for a moment upon a newspaper cutting that he had put aside as a curiosity some days before. It was a paragraph headed "Old Ladies as Mad Motorists," and ran as follows:

> "An unprecedented number of cases of motorists exceeding the speed limit have lately occurred on the Bath Road and other western highways. The extraordinary feature of the case is that in so large a number of cases the offenders appeared to be old ladies of great wealth and respectability who professed to be merely taking their pugs and other pet animals for an airing. They professed that the health of the animal required much more rapid transit through the air than is the case with human beings."

He was gazing at this extract with as much perplexity as on his first perusal, when the Colonel entered with a newspaper in his hand.

"I say," he said, "I think it is getting rather ridiculous. I'm not a revolutionist like you; quite the reverse. But all these rules and regulations are getting beyond all rational discipline. A little while ago they started forbidding all travelling menageries; not, mind you, stipulating for proper conditions for the animals, but forbidding them altogether for some nonsense about the safety of the public. There was a travelling circus stopped near Acton and another on the road to Reading. Crowds of village boys must never see a lion in their lives, because once in fifty years a lion has escaped and been caught again. But that's nothing to what has happened since. Now, if you please, there is such mortal fear of infection that we are to leave the sick to suffer, just as if we were savages. You know those new hospital trains that were started to take patients from the hospitals down to the health resorts. Well, they're not to run after all, it seems, lest by merely taking an invalid of any sort through the open country we should poison the four winds of heaven. If this nonsense goes on, I shall go as mad as Hilary himself."

Hilary Pierce had arrived during this conversation and sat listening to it with a rather curious smile. Somehow the more Hood looked at that smile the more it puzzled him; it puzzled him as much as the newspaper cutting in his hand. He caught himself looking from one to the other, and Pierce smiled in a still more irritating manner.

"You don't look so fierce and fanatical as when we last met, my young friend," observed Owen Hood. "Have you got tired of pigs and police courts? These coercion acts the Colonel's talking about would have roused you to lift the roof off at once."

"Oh, I'm all against the new rules," answered the young man coolly. "I've been very much against them; what you might call up against them. In fact, I've already broken all those new laws and a few more. Could you let me look at that cutting for a moment?"

Hood handed it to him and he nodded, saying:

"Yes; I was arrested for that."

"Arrested for what?"

"Arrested for being a rich and respectable old lady," answered Hilary Pierce; "but I managed to escape that time. It was a fine sight to see the old lady clear a hedge and skedaddle across a meadow"

Hood looked at him under bended brows and his mouth began to work.

"But what's all this about the old lady having a pug or a pet or something?"

"Well, it was very nearly a pug," said Pierce in a dispassionate manner. "I pointed out to everybody that it was, as it were, an approximate pug. I asked if it was just to punish me for a small mistake in spelling."

"I begin to understand," said Hood. "You were again smuggling swine down to your precious Blue Boar, and thought you could rush the frontier in very rapid cars."

"Yes," replied the smuggler placidly "We were quite literally Road-Hogs. I thought at first of dressing the pigs up as millionaires and members of Parliament; but when you come to look close, there's more difference than you would imagine to be possible. It was great fun when they forced me to take my pet out of the wrapping of shawls, and they found what a large pet it was."

"And do I understand," cut in the Colonel, "that it was something like that – with the other laws?"

"The other laws," said Pierce, "are certainly arbitrary, but you do not altogether do them justice. You do not quite appreciate their motive. You do not fully allow for their origin. I may say I trust with modesty, that I was their origin. I not only had the pleasure of breaking those laws, but the pleasure of making them."

"More of your tricks, you mean," said the Colonel; "but why don't the papers say so?"

"The authorities don't want 'em to," answered Pierce. "The authorities won't advertise me, you bet. I've got far too much popular backing for that. When the real revolution happens, it won't be mentioned in the newspapers."

He paused a moment in meditation and then went on.

"When the police searched for my pug and found it was a pig, I started wondering how they could best be stopped from doing it again. It occurred to me they might be shy of a wild pig or a pug that bit them. So, of course, I travelled the next time with dreadfully dangerous animals in cages, warning everybody of the fiercest tigers and panthers that were ever known. When they found it out and didn't want to let it out, they could only fall back on their own tomfoolery of a prohibition wholesale.

Of course, it was the same with my other stunt, about the sick people going to health resorts to be cured of various fashionable and refined maladies. The pigs had a dignified, possibly a rather dull time, in elaborately curtained railway carriages with hospital nurses to wait on them; while I stood outside and assured the railway officials that the cure was a rest cure, and the invalids must on no account be disturbed."

"What a liar you are!" exclaimed Hood in simple admiration.

"Not at all," said Pierce with dignity. "It was quite true that they were going to be cured."

Crane, who had been gazing rather abstractedly out of the window, slowly turned his head and said abruptly: "And how's it going to end? Do you propose to go on doing all these impossible things?"

Pierce sprang to his feet with a resurrection of all the romantic abandon of his vow over the pig-sty.

"Impossible!" he cried. "You don't know what you're saying or how true it is. All I've done so far was possible and prosaic. But I will do an impossible thing. I will do something that is written in all books and rhymes as impossible – something that has passed into a proverb of the impossible. The war is not ended yet; and if you two fellows will post yourselves in the quarry opposite the Blue Boar, on Thursday week at sunset, you will see something so impossible and so self-evident that even the organs of public information will find it hard to hide it."

It was in that part of the steep fall of pinewood where the quarry made a sort of ledge under a roof of pine that two gentlemen of something more than middle age who had not altogether lost the appetite of adventure posted themselves with all the preparations due to a picnic or a practical joke. It was from that place, as from a window looking across the valley, that they saw what seemed more like a vision; what seemed indeed rather like the parody of an apocalypse. The large clearance of the western sky was of a luminous lemon tint, as of pale yellow fading to pale green, while one or two loose clouds on the horizon were of a rose-red and yet richer colours. But the setting sun itself was a cloudless fire, so that a tawny light lay over the whole landscape; and the inn of the Blue Boar standing opposite looked almost like a house of gold. Owen Hood was gazing in his dreamy fashion, and said at last:

"There's an apocalyptic sign in heaven for you to start with. It's a queer thing, but that cloud coming up the valley is uncommonly like the shape of a pig."

"Very like a whale," said Colonel Crane, yawning slightly; but when he turned his eyes in that direction, the eyes were keener. Artists have remarked that a cloud has perspective like anything else; but the perspective of the cloud coming up the valley was curiously solid.

"That's not a cloud," he said sharply, "it's a Zeppelin or something."

The solid shape grew larger and larger; and as it grew more obvious it grew more incredible.

"Saints and angels!" cried Hood suddenly. "Why, it *is* a pig!"

"It's shaped like a pig all right," said the Colonel curtly; and indeed as the great balloon-like form bulked bigger and bigger above its own reflection in the winding river, they could see that the long sausage-shaped Zeppelin body of it had been fantastically decorated with hanging ears and legs, to complete that pantomimic resemblance.

"I suppose it's some more of Hilary's skylarking' observed Hood; "but what is he up to now?"

As the great aerial monster moved up the valley it paused over the inn of the Blue Boar, and something fell fluttering from it like a brightly coloured feather.

"People are coming down in parachutes," said the Colonel shortly.

"They're queer-looking people," remarked his companion, peering under frowning brows, for the level light was dazzling to the eyes. "By George, they're not people at all! They're pigs!"

From that distance, the objects in question had something of the appearance of cherubs in some gaily coloured Gothic picture, with the yellow sky for their gold-leaf background. The parachute apparatus from which they hung and hovered was designed and coloured with the appearance of a great wheel of gorgeously painted plumage, looking more gaudy than ever in the strong evening light that lay over all. The more the two men in the quarry stared at these strange objects, the more certain it seemed that they were indeed pigs; though whether the pigs were dead or alive it was impossible at that distance to say. They looked down into the garden of the inn into which the feathered things were dropping, and they could see the figure of Joan Hardy standing in front of the old pig-sty, with her bird-like head lifted, looking up into the sky.

"Singular present for a young lady," remarked Crane, "but I suppose when our mad young friend does start love-making, he would be likely to give impossible presents."

The eyes of the more poetical Hood were full of larger visions, and he hardly seemed to be listening. But as the sentence ended he seemed to start from a trance and struck his hands together.

"Yes!" he cried in a new voice, "we always come back to that word!"

"Come back to what word?" asked his friend.

"Impossible," answered Owen Hood. "It's the word that runs through his whole life, and ours too for that matter. Don't you see what he has done?"

"I see what he has done all right," answered the Colonel, "but I'm not at all sure I see what you're driving at."

"What we have seen is another impossible thing," said Owen Hood; "a thing that common speech has set up as a challenge; a thing that a thousand rhymes and jokes and phrases have called impossible. We have seen pigs fly."

"It's pretty extraordinary," admitted Crane, "but it's not so extraordinary as their not being allowed to walk."

And they gathered their travelling tackle together and began to descend the steep hill.

In doing so, they descended into a deeper twilight between the stems of the darkling trees; the walls of the valley began to close over them, as it were, and they lost that sense of being in the upper air in a radiant topsy-turvydom of clouds. It was almost as if they had really had a vision; and the voice of Crane came abruptly out of the dusk, almost like that of a doubter when he speaks of a dream.

"The thing I can't understand," he said abruptly, "is how Hilary managed to *do* all that by himself."

"He really is a very wonderful fellow," said Hood. "You told me yourself he did wonders in the War. And though he turns it to these fanatical ends now, it takes as much trouble to do one as the other."

"Takes a devilish lot more trouble to do it alone," said Crane. "In the War there was a whole organization."

"You mean he must be more than a remarkable person," suggested Hood, "a sort of giant with a hundred hands or god with a hundred eyes. Well, a man will work frightfully hard when he wants something very much; even a man who generally looks like a lounging minor poet. And I think I know what it was he wanted. He deserves to get it. It's certainly his hour of triumph."

"Mystery to me all the same," said the Colonel frowning. "Wonder whether he'll ever clear it up." But that part of the mystery was not to be cleared up until many other curious things had come to pass.

Away on another part of the slope Hilary Pierce, new lighted upon the earth like the herald Mercury, leapt down into a red hollow of the quarry and came towards Joan Hardy with uplifted arms.

"This is no time for false modesty" he said. "It is the hour, and I come to you covered with glory – "

"You come covered with mud," she said smiling, "and it's that horrible red mud that takes so long to dry. It's no use trying to brush it till – "

"I bring you the Golden Fleece, or at any rate the Golden Pig-Skin," he cried in lyric ecstasy. "I have endured the labours; I have achieved the quest. I have made the Hampshire Hog as legendary as the Calydonian Boar. They forbade me to drive it on foot, and I drove it in a car, disguised as a pug. They forbade me to bring it in a car, and I brought it in a railway-train, disguised as an invalid. They forbade me to use a railway-train, and I took to the wings of the morning and rose to the uttermost parts of the air; by a way secret and pathless and lonely as the wilful way of love. I have made my romance immortal. I have written your name upon the sky What do you say to me now? I have turned a Pig into a Pegasus. I have done impossible things."

"I know you have," she said, "but somehow I can't help liking you for all that."

"*But* you can't help liking me," he repeated in a hollow voice. "I have stormed heaven, but still I am not so bad. Hercules can be tolerated in spite of his Twelve Labours. St George can be forgiven for killing the Dragon. Woman, is this the way I am treated in the hour of victory; and is this the graceful fashion of an older world? Have you become a New Woman, by any chance? What has your father been doing? What does he say – about us?"

"My father says you are quite mad, of course," she replied, "but he can't help liking you either. He says he doesn't believe in people marrying out of their class; but that if I must marry a gentleman he'd rather it was somebody like you, and not one of the new gentlemen."

"Well, I'm glad I'm an old gentleman, anyhow," he answered somewhat mollified. "But really this prevalence of common sense is getting quite dangerous. Will nothing rouse you all to a little unreality; to saying, so to speak, 'O, for the wings of a pig that I might flee away and be at rest.' What would you say if I turned the world upside down and set my foot upon the sun and moon?"

"I should say," replied Joan Hardy, still smiling, "that you wanted somebody to look after you."

He stared at her for a moment in an almost abstracted fashion as if he had not fully understood; then he laughed uncontrollably, like a man who has seen something very close to him that he knows he is a fool not to have seen before. So a man will fall over something in a game of hiding-and-seeking, and get shaken up with laughter.

"What a bump your mother earth gives you when you fall out of an aeroplane," he said, "especially when your flying ship is only a flying pig. The earth of the real peasants and the real pigs – don't be offended; I assure you the confusion is a compliment. What a thing is horse-sense, and how much finer really than the poetry of Pegasus! And when there is everything else as well that makes the sky clean and the earth kind, beauty and bravery and the lifting of the head – well, you are right enough, Joan. Will you take care of me? Will you stop at home and clip my pig's wings?"

He had caught hold of her by the hands; but she still laughed as she answered:

"Yes – I told you I couldn't help – but you really must let go, Hilary. I can see your friends coming down from the quarry."

As she spoke, indeed, Colonel Crane and Owen Hood could be seen descending the slope and passing through a screen of slender trees towards them.

"Hullo!" said Hilary Pierce cheerfully. "I want you to congratulate me. Joan thinks I'm an awful humbug, and right she is; I am what has been called a happy hypocrite. At least you fellows may think I've been guilty of a bit of fake in this last affair, when I tell you the news. Well, I will confess."

"What news do you mean?" inquired the Colonel with curiosity.

Hilary Pierce grinned and made a gesture over his shoulder to the litter of porcine parachutes, to indicate his last and crowning folly.

"The truth is," he said laughing, "that was only a final firework display to celebrate victory or failure, whichever you choose to call it. There isn't any need to do so any more, because the veto is removed."

"Removed?" exclaimed Hood. "Why on earth is that? It's rather unnerving when lunatics suddenly go sane like that."

"It wasn't anything to do with the lunatics," answered Pierce quietly. "The real change was much higher up, or rather lower down. Anyhow, it was much farther at the back of things, where the Big Businesses are settled by the big people."

"What was the change?" asked the Colonel.

"Old Oates has gone into another business," answered Pierce quietly.

"What on earth has old Oates got to do with it?" asked Hood staring. "Do you mean that Yankee mooning about over medieval ruins?"

"Oh, I know," said Pierce wearily, "I thought he had nothing to do with it; I thought it was the Jews and vegetarians, and the rest; but they're very innocent instruments. The truth is that Enoch Oates is the biggest pork-packer and importer in the world, and he didn't want any competition from our cottagers. And what he says goes, as he would express it. Now, thank God, he's taken up another line."

But if any indomitable reader wishes to know what was the new line Mr Oates pursued and why, it is to be feared that his only course is to await and patiently read the story of The Exclusive Luxury of Enoch Oates; and even before reaching that supreme test, *he* will have to support the recital of The Elusive Companion of Parson White; for these, as has been said, are tales of topsy-turvydom, and they often work backwards.

IV

The Elusive Companion of Parson White

In the scriptures and the chronicles of the League of the Long Bow, or fellowship of foolish persons doing impossible things, it is recorded that Owen Hood, the lawyer, and his friend Crane, the retired Colonel, were partaking one afternoon of a sort of picnic on the river island that had been the first scene of a certain romantic incident in the life of the former, the burden of reading about which has fallen upon the readers in other days. Suffice it to say that the island had been devoted by Mr Hood to his hobby of angling, and that the meal then in progress was a somewhat early interruption of the same leisurely pursuit. The two old cronies had a third companion, who, though considerably younger, was not only a companion but a friend. He was a light-haired, lively young man, with rather a wild eye, known by the name of Pierce, whose wedding to the daughter of the innkeeper of the Blue Boar the others had only recently attended.

He was an aviator and given to many other forms of skylarking. The two older men had eccentric tastes of their own; but there is always a difference between the eccentricity of an elderly man who defies the world and the enthusiasm of a younger man who hopes to alter it. The old gentleman may be willing, in a sense, to stand on his head; but he does not hope, as the boy does, to stand the world on its head. With a young man like Hilary Pierce it was the world itself that was to be turned upside-down; and that was a game at which his more grizzled companions could only look on, as at a child they loved [who was] playing with a big coloured balloon.

Perhaps it was this sense of a division by time, altering the tone, though not the fact, of friendship, which sent the mind of one of the older men back to the memory of an older friend. He remembered he had had a letter that morning from the only contemporary of his who could fitly have made a fourth to their party. Owen Hood drew the letter from his pocket with a smile that wrinkled his long, humorous, cadaverous face.

"By the way I forgot to tell you," he said, "I had a letter from White yesterday."

The bronzed visage of the Colonel was also seamed with the external signs of a soundless chuckle.

"Read it yet?" he asked.

"Yes," replied the lawyer; "the hieroglyphic was attacked with fresh vigour after breakfast this morning, and the clouds and mysteries of yesterday's laborious hours seemed to be rolled away. Some portions of the cuneiform still await an expert translation; but the sentences themselves appear to be in the original English."

"Very original English," snorted Colonel Crane.

"Yes, our friend is an original character," replied Hood. "Vanity tempts me to hint that he is our friend because he has an original taste in friends. The habit of his of putting the pronoun on the first page and the noun on the next has brightened many winter evenings for me. You haven't met our friend White, have you?" he added to Pierce. "That is a shock that still threatens you."

"Why, what's the matter with him?" inquired Pierce.

"Nothing," observed Crane in his more staccato style. "Has a taste for starting a letter with 'Yours Truly' and ending it with 'Dear Sir'; that's all."

"I should rather like to hear that letter," observed the young man.

"So you shall," answered Hood, "there's nothing confidential in it; and if there were, you wouldn't find it out merely by reading it. The Rev Wilding White, called by some of his critics 'Wild White,' is one of those country parsons, to be found in corners of the English countryside, of whom their old college friends usually think in order to wonder what the devil their parishioners think of them. As a matter of fact, my dear Hilary, he was rather like you when he was your age; and what in the world you would be like as a vicar in the Church of England, aged fifty, might at first stagger the imagination; but the problem might be solved by supposing you would be like him. But I only hope you will have a more lucid style in letter-writing. The old boy is always in such a state of excitement about something that it comes out anyhow."

It has been said elsewhere that these tales are, in some sense, of necessity told tail-foremost, and certainly the letter of the Rev Wilding White was a document suited to such a scheme of narrative. It was written in what had once been a good hand-writing of the bolder sort, but which had degenerated through excessive energy and haste into an illegible scrawl. It appeared to run as follows:

> " 'My dear Owen, – My mind is quite made up; though I know the sort of legal long-winded things you will say against it; I know especially one thing a leathery old lawyer like you is bound to say; but as a matter of fact even you can't say it in a case like this, because the timber came from the other end of the county and had nothing whatever to do with him or any of his flunkeys and sycophants. Besides, I did it all myself with a little

assistance I'll tell you about later; and even in these days I should be surprised to hear *that* sort of assistance could be anything but a man's own affair. I defy you and all your parchments to maintain that it comes under the Game Laws. You won't mind me talking like this; I know jolly well you'd think you were acting as a friend; but I think the time has come to speak plainly' "

"Quite right," said the Colonel.

"Yes," said young Pierce, with a rather vague expression, "I'm glad he feels that the time has come to speak plainly."

"Quite so," observed the lawyer dryly; "he continues as follows":

" 'I've got a lot to tell you about the new arrangement, which works much better even than I hoped. I was afraid at first it would really be an encumbrance, as you know it's always supposed to be. But there are more things, and all the rest of it, and God fulfils himself; and so on and so on. It gives one quite a weird Asiatic feeling sometimes.' "

"Yes," said the Colonel, "it does."

"What does?" asked Pierce, sitting up suddenly, like one who can bear no more.

"You are not used to the epistolary method," said Hood indulgently; "you haven't got into the swing of the style. It goes on":

" 'Of course, he's a big pot down here, and all sorts of skunks are afraid of him and pretend to boycott me. Nobody could expect anything else of those pineapple people, but I confess I was surprised at Parkinson. Sally of course is as sound as ever; but she goes to Scotland a good deal and you can't blame her. Sometimes I'm left pretty severely alone, but I'm not downhearted; you'll probably laugh if I tell you that Snowdrop is really a very intelligent companion.' "

"I confess I am long past laughter," said Hilary Pierce sadly; "but I rather wish I knew who Snowdrop is."

"Child, I suppose," said the Colonel shortly.

"Yes; I suppose it must be a child," said Pierce. "Has he any children?"

"No," said the Colonel. "Bachelor."

"I believe he was in love with a lady in those parts and never married in consequence," said Hood. "It would be quite on the lines of fiction and film-drama if Snowdrop were the daughter of the lady, when she had married Another. But there seems to be something more about Snowdrop, that little sunbeam in the house":

" 'Snowdrop tries to enter our ways, as they always do; but, of course, it would be awkward if she played tricks. How alarmed they would all be if she took it into her head to walk about on two legs, like everybody else.' "

"Nonsense!" ejaculated Colonel Crane. "Can't be a child – talking about it walking about on two legs."

"After all," said Pierce thoughtfully, "a little girl does walk about on two legs."

"Bit startling if she walked about on three," said Crane.

"If my learned brother will allow me," said Hood, in his forensic manner, "would he describe the fact of a little girl walking on two legs as alarming?"

"A little girl is always alarming," replied Pierce.

"I've come to the conclusion myself," went on Hood, "that Snowdrop must be a pony. It seems a likely enough name for a pony. I thought at first it was a dog or a cat, but alarming seems a strong word even for a dog or a cat sitting up to beg. But a pony on its hind legs might be a little alarming, especially when you're riding it. Only I can't fit this view in with the next sentence: 'I've taught her to reach down the things I want.' "

"Lord!" cried Pierce. "It's a monkey!"

"That," replied Hood, "had occurred to me as possibly explaining the weird Asiatic atmosphere. But a monkey on two legs is even less unusual than a dog on two legs. Moreover, the reference to Asiatic mystery seems really to refer to something else and not to any animal at all. For he ends up by saying:

> " 'I feel now as if my mind were moving in much larger and more ancient spaces of time or eternity; and as if what I thought at first was an oriental atmosphere was only an atmosphere of the orient in the sense of dayspring and the dawn. It has nothing to do with the stagnant occultism of decayed Indian cults; it is something that unites a real innocence with the immensities, a power as of the mountains with the purity of snow. This vision does not violate my own religion, but rather reinforces it; but I cannot help feeling that I have larger views. I hope in two senses to preach liberty in these parts. So I may live to falsify the proverb after all.' "

"That," added Hood, folding up the letter, "is the only sentence in the whole thing that conveys anything to my mind. As it happens, we have all three of us lived to falsify proverbs."

Hilary Pierce had risen to his feet with the restless action that went best with his alert figure. "Yes," he said; "I suppose we can all three of us say we have lived for adventures, or had some curious ones anyhow. And to tell you the truth, the adventure feeling has come on me very strong at this very minute. I've got the detective fever about that parson of yours. I should like to get at the meaning of that letter, as if it were a cipher about buried treasure."

Then he added more gravely: "And if, as I gather, your clerical friend is really a friend worth having, I do seriously advise you to keep an eye on him just now. Writing letters upside-down is all very well, and I shouldn't be alarmed about that. Lots of people think they've explained things in previous letters they never wrote. I don't think it matters who Snowdrop is, or what sort of children or animals he chooses to be fond of. That's all being eccentric in the good old English fashion, like poetical tinkers and mad squires. You're both of you eccentric in that sort of way, and it's one of the things I like about you. But just because I naturally knock about more among the new people, I see something of the new eccentricities. And believe me, they're not half so nice as the old ones. I'm a student of scientific aviation, which is a new thing itself, and I like it. But there's a sort of spiritual aviation that I don't like at all."

"Sorry" observed Crane. "Really no notion of what you're talking about."

"Of course you haven't," answered Pierce with engaging candour; "that's another thing I like about you. But I don't like the way your clerical friend talks about new visions and larger religions and light and liberty from the East. I've heard a good many people talk like that, and they were mountebanks or the dupes of mountebanks. And I'll tell you another thing. It's a long shot even with the long bow we used to talk about. It's a pretty wild guess even in this rather wild business. But I have a creepy sort of feeling that if you went down to his house and private parlour to see Snowdrop, you'd be surprised at what you saw."

"What should we see?" asked the Colonel, staring.

"You'd see nothing at all," replied the young man.

"What on earth do you mean?"

"I mean," replied Pierce, "that you'd find Mr White talking to somebody who didn't seem to be there."

Hilary Pierce, fired by his detective fever, made a good many more inquiries about the Rev Wilding White, both of his two old friends and elsewhere.

One long legal conversation with Owen Hood did indeed put him in possession of the legal outline of certain matters, which might be said to throw a light on some parts of the strange letter, and which might in time even be made to throw a light on the rest. White was the vicar of a parish lying deep in the western parts of Somersetshire, where the principal landowner was a certain Lord Arlington. And in this case there had been a quarrel between the squire and the parson, of a more revolutionary sort than is common in the case of parsons. The clergyman intensely resented that irony or anomaly which has caused so much discontent among tenants in Ireland and throughout the world; the fact that improvements or constructive work actually done by the tenant only pass into the possession of the landlord. He had considerably improved a house that he himself rented from the squire, but in some kind of crisis of defiance or renunciation, he had quitted this more official residence bag and baggage, and built himself a sort of wooden lodge or bungalow on a small hill or mound that rose amid woods on the extreme edge of the same grounds. This quarrel about the claim of the tenant to his own work was evidently the meaning of certain phrases in the letter – such as the timber coming from the other end of the county, the sort of work being a man's own affair, and the general allusion to somebody's flunkeys or sycophants who attempted to boycott the discontented tenant. But it was not quite so clear whether the allusions to a new arrangement, and how it worked, referred to the bungalow or to the other and more elusive mystery of the presence of Snowdrop.

One phrase in the letter he found to have been repeated in many places and to many persons without becoming altogether clear in the process. It was the sentence that ran: "I was afraid at first it would really be an encumbrance, as you know it's always supposed to be." Both Colonel Crane and Owen Hood, and also several other persons whom he met later in his investigations, were agreed in saying that Mr White had used some expression indicating that he had entangled himself with something troublesome or at least useless; something that he did not want. None of them could remember the exact words he had used; but all could state in general terms that it referred to some sort of negative nuisance or barren responsibility. This could hardly refer to Snowdrop, of whom he always wrote in terms of tenderness as if she were a baby or a kitten. It seemed hard to believe it could refer to the house he had built entirely to suit himself. It seemed as if there must be some third thing in his muddled existence, which loomed vaguely in the background through the vapour of his confused correspondence.

Colonel Crane snapped his fingers with a mild irritation in trying to recall a trifle. "He said it was a – you know, I've forgotten the word – a botheration or embarrassment. But then he's always in a state of botheration and embarrassment. I didn't tell you, by the way, that I had a letter from him too. Came the day after I heard yours. Shorter, and perhaps a little plainer." And he handed the letter to Hood, who read it out slowly:

> " 'I never knew the old British populace, here in Avalon itself; could be so broken down by squires and sneaking lawyers. Nobody dared help me move my house again; said it was illegal and they were afraid of the police. But Snowdrop helped, and we carted it all away in two or three journeys; took it right clean off the old fool's land altogether this time. I fancy the old fool will have to admit there are things in this world he wasn't prepared to believe in.' "

"But look here," began Hood as if impulsively, and then stopped and spoke more slowly and carefully. "I don't understand this; I think it's extremely odd. I don't mean odd for an ordinary person, but odd for an odd person; odd for this odd person. I know White better than either of you can, and I can tell you that, though he tells a tale anyhow, the tale is always true. He's rather precise and pedantic when you do come to the facts; these litigious quarrelsome people always are. He would do extraordinary things, but he wouldn't make them out more extraordinary than they were. I mean he's the sort of man who might break all the squire's windows, but he wouldn't say he'd broken six when he'd broken five. I've always found when I'd got to the meaning of those mad letters that it was quite true. But how can this be true? How could Snowdrop, whatever she is, have moved a whole house, or old White either?"

"I suppose you know what I think," said Pierce. "I told you that Snowdrop, whatever else she is, is invisible. I'm certain your friend has gone Spiritualist, and Snowdrop is the name of a spirit, or a control, or whatever they call it. The spirit would say, of course, that it was mere child's play to throw the house from one end of the county to the other. But if this unfortunate gentleman believes himself to have been thrown, house and all, in that fashion, I'm very much afraid he's begun really to suffer from delusions."

The faces of the two older men looked suddenly much older, perhaps for the first time they looked old. The young man seeing their dolorous expression was warmed and fired to speak quickly.

"Look here," he said hastily, "I'll go down there myself and find out what I can for you. I'll go this afternoon."

"Train journey takes ages," said the Colonel, shaking his head. "Other end of nowhere. Told me yourself you had an appointment at the Air Ministry tomorrow."

"Be there in no time," replied Pierce cheerfully. "I'll fly down."

And there was something in the lightness and youth of his vanishing gesture that seemed really like Icarus spurning the earth, the first man to mount upon wings.

Perhaps this literally flying figure shone the more vividly in their memories because, when they saw it again, it was in a subtle sense changed. When the other two next saw Hilary Pierce on the steps of the Air Ministry, they were conscious that his manner was a little quieter, but his wild eye rather wilder than usual. They adjourned to a neighbouring restaurant and talked of trivialities while luncheon was served; but the Colonel, who was a keen observer, was sure that Pierce had suffered some sort of shock, or at least some sort of check. While they were considering what to say Pierce himself said abruptly, staring at a mustard-pot on the table:

"What do you think about spirits?"

"Never touch 'em," said the Colonel. "Sound port never hurt anybody."

"I mean the other sort," said Pierce. "Things like ghosts and all that."

"I don't know," said Owen Hood. "The Greek for it is agnosticism. The Latin for it is ignorance. But have you really been dealing with ghosts and spirits down at poor White's parsonage?"

"I don't know," said Pierce gravely.

"You don't mean you really think you saw something!" cried Hood sharply.

"There goes the agnostic!" said Pierce with a rather weary smile. "The minute the agnostic hears a bit of real agnosticism he shrieks out that it's superstition. I say I don't know whether it was a spirit. I also say I don't know what the devil else it was if it wasn't. In plain words, I went down to that place convinced that poor White had got some sort of delusions. Now I wonder whether it's I that have got the delusions."

He paused a moment and then went on in a more collected manner:

"But I'd better tell you all about it. To begin with, I don't admit it as an explanation, but it's only fair to allow for it as a fact – that all that part of the world seems to be full of that sort of thing. You know how the glamour of Glastonbury lies over all that land and the lost tomb of King Arthur and time when he shall return and the prophecies of Merlin and all the rest. To begin with, the village they call Ponder's End ought to be called World's End; it gives one the impression of being somewhere west of the sunset. And then the parsonage is quite a long way west of the parish, in large neglected grounds fading into pathless woods and hills; I mean the old empty rectory that our wild friend has evacuated. It stood there a cold empty shell of flat classical architecture, as hollow as one of those classical temples they used to stick up in country seats. But White must have done some sort of parish work there, for I found a great big empty shed in the grounds – that sort of thing that's used for a schoolroom or drill-hall or what not. But not a sign of him or his work can be seen there now. I've said it's a long way west of the village that you come at last to the old house. Well, it's a long way west of that that you come to the new house – if you come to it at all. As for me, I came and I came not, as in some old riddle of Merlin. But you shall hear.

"I had come down about sunset in a meadow near Ponder's End, and I did the rest of the journey on foot, for I wanted to see things in detail. This was already difficult as it was growing dusk, and I began to fear I should find nothing of importance before nightfall. I had asked a question or two of the villagers about the vicar and his new self-made vicarage. They were very reticent about the former, but I gathered that the latter stood at the extreme edge of his original grounds on a hill rising out of a thicket of wood. In the increasing darkness it was difficult to find the place, but I came on it at last, in a place where a fringe of forest ran along under the low brows of a line of rugged cliffs, such as sometimes break the curves of great downlands. I seemed to be descending a thickly wooded slope, with a sea of tree-tops below me, and out of that sea, like an island, rose the dome of the isolated hill; and I could faintly see the building on it, darker against the dark-clouded sky. For a moment a faint line of light from the masked moon showed me a little more of its shape, which seemed singularly simple and airy in its design. Against that pallid gleam stood four strong columns, with the bulk of building apparently lifted above them; but it produced a queer impression, as if this Christian priest had built for his final home a heathen temple of the winds. As I leaned forward, peering at it, I overbalanced myself and slid rapidly down the steep thicket into the darkest entrails of the wood. From there I could see nothing of the pillared house or temple or whatever it was on the hill; the thick woods had swallowed me up literally like a sea, and I groped for what must have been nearly half an hour amid tangled roots and low branches, in that double darkness of night and shadow, before I found my feet slipping on the opposite slope and began to climb the hill on the top of which the temple stood. It was very difficult climbing, of course, through a network of briars and branching trees, and it was some little time afterwards that I burst through the last screen of foliage and came out upon the bare hilltop.

"Yes; upon the bare hilltop. Rank grasses grew upon it, and the wind blew them about like hair on a head; but for any trace of anything else, that green dome was as bare as a skull. There was no sign or shadow of the building I had seen there a little time before; it had vanished like a fairy palace. A broad track broken through the woods seemed to lead up to it, so far as I could make out in that obscurity; but there was no trace of the building to which it led. And when I saw that, I gave up. Something told me I should find out no more; perhaps I had some shaken sense that there were things past finding out. I retraced my steps, descending the hill as best I might; but when I was again swallowed up in that leafy sea, something happened that, for an instant, turned me cold as stone. An unearthly noise, like long hooting laughter, rang out in vast volume over the forest and rose to the stars. It was no noise to which I could put a name; it was certainly no noise I had ever heard before; it bore some sort of resemblance to the neighing of a horse immensely magnified; yet it might have been half human, and there was triumph in it and derision.

"I will tell you one more thing I learnt before I left those parts. I left them at once, partly because I really had an appointment early this morning, as I told you; partly also, I think, because I felt you had the right to know at once what sort of things were to be faced. I was alarmed when I thought your friend was tormented with imaginary bogies; I am not less alarmed if he had got mixed up with real ones. Anyhow, before I left that village I had told one man what I had seen, and he told me he had seen it also. But he had seen it actually moving, in dusk turning to dark; the whole great house, with its high columns, moving across the fields like a great ship sailing on land."

Owen Hood sat up suddenly, with awakened eyes, and struck the table.

"Look here," he cried, with a new ring in his voice, "we must all go down to Ponder's End and bring this business to a finish."

"Do you think you will bring it to a finish?" asked Pierce gloomily; "or can you tell what sort of finish?"

"Yes," replied Hood resolutely. "I think I can finish it, and I think I know what the finish will be. The truth is, my friend, I think I understand the whole thing now. And as I told you before, Wilding White, so far from being deluded by imaginary bogies, is a gentleman very exact in his statements. In this matter he has been very exact. That has been the whole mystery about him – that he has been very much too exact."

"What on earth do you mean by that?" asked Pierce.

"I mean," said the lawyer, "that I have suddenly remembered the phrase he used. It was very exact; it was dull, deadly, literal truth. But I can be exact, too, at times, and just now I should like to look at a timetable."

They found the village of Ponder's End in a condition as comically incongruous as could well be with the mystical experiences of Mr Hilary Pierce. When we talk of such places as sleepy, we forget that they are very wide-awake about their own affairs, and especially on their own festive occasions. Piccadilly Circus looks much the same on Christmas Day or any other; but the market-place of a country town or village looks very different on the day of a fair or a bazaar. And Hilary Pierce, who had first come down there to find in a wood at midnight the riddle that he thought worthy of Merlin, came down the second time to find himself plunged suddenly into the middle of the bustling bathos of a jumble sale. It was one of those bazaars to provide bargains for the poor, at which all sorts of odds and ends are sold off. But it was treated as a sort of fête, and highly-coloured posters and handbills announced its nature on every side. The bustle seemed to be dominated by a tall dark lady of distinguished appearance, whom Owen Hood, rather to the surprise of his companions, hailed as an old acquaintance and managed to draw aside for a private talk. She had appeared to have her hands full at the bazaar; nevertheless, her talk with Hood was rather a long one. Pierce heard only the last words of it:

"Oh, he promised he was bringing something for the sale. I assure you he always keeps his word."

All Hood said when he rejoined his companion was: "That's the lady White was going to marry. I think I know now why things went wrong, and I hope they may go right. But there seems to be another bother. You see that clump of clod-hopping policemen over there, inspector and all. It seems they're waiting for White. Says he's broken the law in taking his house off the land, and that he has always eluded them. I hope there won't be a scene when he turns up."

If this was Mr Hood's hope, it was ill-founded and destined to disappointment. A scene was but a faint description of what was in store for that hopeful gentleman. Within ten minutes the greater part of the company were in a world in which the sun and the moon seemed to have turned topsy-turvy and the last limit of unlikelihood had been reached. Pierce had imagined he was very near that limit of the imagination when he groped after the vanishing temple in the dark forest. But nothing he had seen in that darkness and solitude was so fantastic as what he saw next in broad daylight and in a crowd.

At one extreme edge of the crowd there was a sudden movement – a wave of recoil and wordless cries. The next moment it had swept like a wind over the whole populace, and hundreds of faces were turned in one direction – in the direction of the road that descended by a gradual slope towards the woods that fringed the vicarage grounds. Out of these woods at the foot of the hill had emerged something that might from its size have been a large light grey omnibus. But it was not an omnibus. It scaled the slope so swiftly, in great strides, that it became instantly self-evident what it was. It was an elephant, whose monstrous form was moulded in grey and silver in the sunlight, and on whose back sat very erect a vigorous middle-aged gentleman in black clerical attire, with blanched hair and a rather fierce aquiline profile that glanced proudly to left and right.

The police inspector managed to make one step forward, and then stood like a statue. The vicar, on his vast steed, sailed into the middle of the market-place as serenely as if he had been the master of a familiar circus. He pointed in triumph to one of the red and blue posters on the wall, which bore the traditional title of "White Elephant Sale."

"You see I've kept my word," he said to the lady in a loud, cheerful voice. "I've brought a white elephant."

The next moment he had waved his hand hilariously in another direction, having caught sight of Hood and Crane in the crowd.

"Splendid of you to come!" he called out. "Only you were in the secret. I told you I'd got a white elephant."

"So he did," said Hood, "only it never occurred to us that the elephant was an elephant and not a metaphor. So that's what he meant by Asiatic atmosphere and snow and mountains. And that's what the big shed was really for."

"Look here," said the inspector, recovering from his astonishment and breaking in on these felicitations. "I don't understand all these games, but it's my business to ask a few questions. Sorry to say it, sir, but you've ignored our notifications and evaded our attempts to – "

"Have I?" inquired Mr White brightly. "Have I really evaded you? Well, well, perhaps I have. An elephant is such a standing temptation to evasion, to evanescence, to fading away like a dewdrop. Like a snowdrop perhaps would be more appropriate. Come on, Snowdrop."

The last word came smartly, and he gave a smart smack to the huge head of the pachyderm. Before the inspector could move or anyone had realized what had happened, the whole big bulk had pitched forward with a plunge like a cataract and went in great whirling strides, the crowd scattering before it. The police had not come provided for elephants, which are rare in those parts. Even if they had overtaken it on bicycles, they would have found it difficult to climb it on bicycles. Even if they had had revolvers, they had omitted to conceal about their persons anything in the way of big-game rifles. The white monster vanished rapidly up the long white road, so rapidly that when it dwindled to a small object and disappeared, people could hardly believe that such a prodigy had ever been present, or that their eyes had not been momentarily bewitched. Only, as it disappeared in the distance, Pierce heard once more the high nasal trumpeting noise which, in the eclipse of night, had seemed to fill the forest with fear.

It was at a subsequent meeting in London that Crane and Pierce had an opportunity of learning, more or less, the true story of the affair, in the form of another letter from the parson to the lawyer.

"Now that we know the secret," said Pierce cheerfully, "even his account of it ought to be quite clear."

"Quite clear," replied Hood calmly. "His letter begins, 'Dear Owen, I am really tremendously grateful in spite of all I used to say against leather and about horse-hair.' "

"About what?" asked Pierce.

"Horse-hair," said Hood with severity. "He goes on, 'The truth is they thought they could do what they liked with me because I always boasted that I hadn't got one, and never wanted to have one; but when they found I had got one, and I must really say a jolly good one, of course it was all quite different.' "

Pierce had his elbows up on the table, and his fingers thrust up into his loose yellow hair. He had rather the appearance of holding his head on. He was muttering to himself very softly, like a schoolboy learning a lesson.

"He had got one, but he didn't want one, and he hadn't got one and he had a jolly good one."

"One what?" asked Crane irritably "Seems like a missing word competition."

"I've got the prize," observed Hood placidly. "The missing word is 'solicitor.' What he means is that the police took liberties with him because they knew he would not have a lawyer. And he is perfectly right; for when I took the matter up on his behalf; I soon found that they had put themselves on the wrong side of the law at least as much as he had. In short, I was able to extricate him from this police business; hence his hearty if not lucid gratitude. But he goes on to talk about something rather more personal; and I think it really has been a rather interesting case, if he does not exactly shine as a narrator of it. As I dare say you noticed, I did know something of the lady whom our eccentric friend went courting years ago, rather in the spirit of Sir Roger de Coverly when he went courting the widow. She is a Miss Julia Drake, daughter of a country gentleman. I hope you won't misunderstand me if I say that she is a rather formidable lady. She is really a thoroughly good sort; but that air of the black-browed Juno she has about her does correspond to some real qualities. She is one of those people who can manage big enterprises, and the bigger they are the happier she is. When that sort of force functions within the limits of a village or a small valley, the impact is sometimes rather overpowering. You saw her managing the White Elephant Sale at Ponder's End. Well, if it had been literally an army of wild elephants, it would hardly have been on too large a scale for her tastes. In that sense, I may say that our friend's white elephant was not so much of a white elephant. I mean that in that sense it was not so much of an irrelevancy and hardly even a surprise. But in another way, it was a very great relief."

"You're getting nearly as obscure as he is," remonstrated Pierce. "What is all this mysterious introduction leading up to? What do you mean?"

"I mean," replied the lawyer, "that experience has taught me a little secret about very practical public characters like that lady. It sounds a paradox; but those practical people are often more morbid than theoretical people. They are capable of acting; but they are also capable of brooding when they are not acting. Their very stoicism makes too sentimental a secret of their sentimentalism. They misunderstand those they love; and make a mystery of the misunderstanding. They suffer in silence; a horrid habit. In short, they can do everything; but they don't know how to do nothing. Theorists, happy people who do nothing, like our friend Pierce – "

"Look here," cried the indignant Pierce. "I should like to know what the devil you mean? I've broken more law than you ever read in your life. If this psychological lecture is the new lucidity, give me Mr White."

"Oh, very well," replied Hood, "if you prefer his text to my exposition, he describes the same situation as follows: 'I ought to be grateful, being perfectly happy after all this muddle; I suppose one ought to be careful about nomenclature; but it never even occurred to me that her nose would be out of joint. Rather funny to be talking about noses, isn't it, for I suppose really it was her rival's nose that figured most prominently. Think of having a rival with a nose like that to turn up at you! Talk about a spire pointing to the stars – ' "

"I think," said Crane, interposing mildly, "that it would be better if you resumed your duties as official interpreter. What was it that you were going to say about the lady who brooded over misunderstandings?"

"I was going to say," replied the lawyer, "that when I first came upon that crowd in the village, and saw that tall figure and dark strong face dominating it in the old way, my mind went back to a score of things I remembered about her in the past. Though we have not met for ten years, I knew from the first glimpse of her face that she had been worrying, in a powerful secretive sort of way; worrying about something she didn't understand and would not inquire about. I remember long ago, when she was an ordinary fox-hunting squire's daughter and White was one of Sydney Smith's wild curates, how she sulked for two months over a mistake about a postcard that could have been explained in two minutes. At least it could have been explained by anybody except White. But you will understand that if he tried to explain the postcard on another postcard, the results may not have been luminous, let alone radiant."

"But what has all this to do with noses?" inquired Pierce.

"Don't you understand yet?" asked Hood with a smile. "Don't you know who was the rival with the long nose?"

He paused for a moment and then continued. "It occurred to me as soon as I had guessed at the nature of the nose which may certainly be called the main feature of the story. An elusive, flexible and insinuating nose, the serpent of their Eden. Well, they seem to have returned to their Eden now; and I have no doubt it will be all right; for it is when people are separated that these sort of secrets spring up between them. After all, it was a mystery to us and we cannot be surprised if it was a mystery to her."

"A good deal of this talk is still rather a mystery to me," remarked Pierce, "though I admit it is getting a little clearer. You mean that the point that has just been cleared up is – "

"The point about Snowdrop," replied Hood. "We thought of a pony, and a monkey and a baby, and a good many other things that Snowdrop might possibly be. But we never thought of the interpretation which was the first to occur to the lady."

There was silence, and then Crane laughed in an internal fashion.

"Well, I don't blame her," he said. "One could hardly expect a lady of any delicacy to deduce an elephant."

"It's an extraordinary business, when you come to think of it," said Pierce. "Where did he get the elephant?"

"He says something about that too," said Hood, referring to the letter. "He says, 'I may be a quarrelsome fellow. But quarrels sometimes do good. And though it wasn't actually one of Captain Pierce's caravans – ' "

"No, hang it all!" cried Pierce. "This is really too much! To see one's own name entangled in such hieroglyphics – it reminds me of seeing it in a Dutch paper during the war; and wondering whether all the other words were terms of abuse."

"I think I can explain," answered Hood patiently. "I assure you the reverend gentleman is not taking liberties with your name in a merely irresponsible spirit. As I told you before, he is strictly truthful when you get at the facts, though they may be difficult to get at. Curiously enough, there really is a connexion. I sometimes think there is a connexion beyond coincidence running through all our adventures; a purpose in these unconscious practical jokes. It seems rather eccentric to make friends with a white elephant – "

"Rather eccentric to make friends with us," said the Colonel. "We are a set of white elephants."

"As a matter of fact," said the lawyer, "this particular last prank of the parson really did arise out of the last prank of our friend Pierce."

"Me!" said Pierce in surprise. "Have I been producing elephants without knowing it?"

"Yes," replied Hood. "You remember when you were smuggling pigs in defiance of the regulations, you indulged (I regret to say) in a deception of putting them in cages and pretending you were travelling with a menagerie of dangerous animals. The consequence was, you remember, that the authorities forbade menageries altogether. Our friend White took up the case of a travelling circus being stopped in his town as a case of gross oppression; and when they had to break it up, he took over the elephant."

"Sort of small payment for his services, I suppose," said Crane. "Curious idea, taking a tip in the form of an elephant."

"He might not have done it if he'd known what it involved," said Hood. "As I say, he was a quarrelsome fellow, with all his good points."

There was a silence, and then Pierce said in a musing manner: "It's odd it should be the sequel of my little pig adventure. A sort of reversal of the *parturiunt montes*; I put in a little pig and it brought forth an elephant?"

"It will bring forth more monsters yet," said Owen Hood. "We have not seen all the sequels of your adventures as a swineherd."

But touching the other monsters or monstrous events so produced the reader has already been warned – nay, threatened – that they are involved in the narrative called The Exclusive Luxury of Enoch Oates, and for the moment the threat must hang like thunder in the air.

V

The Exclusive Luxury Of Enoch Oates

"Since the Colonel ate his hat the Lunatic Asylum has lacked a background."

The conscientious scribe cannot but be aware that the above sentence, standing alone and without reference to previous matters, may not entirely explain itself. Anyone trying the experiment of using that sentence for practical social purposes; tossing that sentence lightly as a greeting to a passer-by; sending that sentence as a telegram to a total stranger; whispering that sentence hoarsely into the ear of the nearest policeman, and so on, will find that its insufficiency as a full and final statement is generally felt. With no morbid curiosity, with no exaggerated appetite for omniscience, men will want to know more about this statement before acting upon it. And the only way of explaining it, and the unusual circumstances in which it came to be said, is to pursue the doubling and devious course of these narratives, and return to a date very much earlier, when men now more than middle-aged were quite young.

It was in the days when the Colonel was not the Colonel, but only Jimmy Crane, a restless youth tossed about by every wind of adventure, but as yet as incapable of discipline as of dressing for dinner. It was in days before Robert Owen Hood, the lawyer, had ever begun to study the law and had only got so far as to abolish it; coming down to the club every night with a new plan for a revolution to turn all earthly tribunals upside down. It was in days before Wilding White settled down as a country parson, returning to the creed though not the conventions of his class and country; when he was still ready to change his religion once a week, turning up sometimes in the costume of a monk and sometimes of a mufti, and sometimes in what he declared to be the original vestments of a Druid, whose religion was shortly to be resumed by the whole British people. It was in days when their young friend Hilary Pierce, the aviator, was still anticipating aviation by flying a small kite. In short, it was early in the lives even of the elders of the group that they had founded a small social club, in which their long friendships had flourished. The club had to have some sort of name, and the more thoughtful and detached among them, who saw the club steadily and saw it whole, considered the point with ripe reflection, and finally called their little society the Lunatic Asylum.

"We might all stick straws in our hair for dinner, as the Romans crowned themselves with roses for the banquet," observed Hood. "It would correspond to dressing for dinner; I don't know what else we could do to vary the vulgar society trick of all wearing the same sort of white waistcoats."

"All wearing strait waistcoats, I suppose," said Crane.

"We might each dine separately in a padded cell, if it comes to that," said Hood; "but there seems to be something lacking in it considered as a social evening."

Here Wilding White, who was then in a monastic phase, intervened eagerly. He explained that in some monasteries a monk of particular holiness was allowed to become a hermit in an inner cell, and proposed a similar arrangement at the club. Hood, with his more mellow rationalism, intervened with a milder amendment. He suggested that a large padded chair should represent the padded cell, and be reserved like a throne for the loftiest of the lunatics.

"Do not," he said gently and earnestly, "do not let us be divided by jealousies and petty ambitions. Do not let us dispute among ourselves which shall be the dottiest in the domain of the dotty. Perhaps one will appear worthier than us all, more manifestly and magnificently weak in the head; for him let the padded throne stand empty."

Jimmy Crane had said no more after his brief suggestion, but was pacing the room like a polar bear, as he generally did when there came upon him a periodical impulse to go off after things like polar bears. He was the wildest of all those wild figures so far as the scale of his adventures was concerned, constantly vanishing to the ends of the earth nobody knew why, and turning up again nobody knew how. He had a hobby, even in his youth, that made his outlook seem even stranger than the bewildering successive philosophies of his friend White. He had an enthusiasm for the myths of savages, and while White was balancing the relative claims of Buddhism and Brahminism, Crane would boldly declare his preference for the belief that a big fish ate the sun every night, or that the whole cosmos was created by cutting up a giant. Moreover, there was with all this something indefinable but in some way more serious about Crane even in these days. There was much that was merely boyish about the blind impetuosity of Wilding White, with his wild hair and eager aquiline face. He was evidently one who might (as he said) learn the secret of Isis, but would be quite incapable of keeping it to himself. The long, legal face of Owen Hood had already learned to laugh at most things, if not to laugh loudly. But in Crane there was something more hard and militant like steel, and as he proved afterwards in the affair of the hat, he could keep a secret even when it was a joke. So that when he finally went off on a long tour round the world, with the avowed intention of studying all the savages he could find, nobody tried to stop him. He went off in a startlingly shabby suit, with a faded sash instead of a waistcoat, and with no luggage in particular, except a large revolver slung round him in a case like a field-glass, and a big, green umbrella that he flourished resolutely as he walked.

"Well, he'll come back a queerer figure than he went, I suppose," said Wilding White.

"He couldn't," answered Hood, the lawyer, shaking his head. "I don't believe all the devil-worship in Africa could make him any madder than he is."

"But he's going to America first, isn't he?" said the other.

"Yes," said Hood. "He's going to America, but not to see the Americans. He would think the Americans very dull compared with the American Indians. Possibly he will come back in feathers and war-paint."

"He'll come back scalped, I suppose," said White hopefully. "I suppose being scalped is all the rage in the best Red Indian society?"

"Then he's working round by the South Sea Islands," said Hood. "They don't scalp people there; they only stew them in pots."

"He couldn't very well come back stewed," said White, musing. "Does it strike you, Owen, that we should hardly be talking nonsense like this if we hadn't a curious faith that a fellow like Crane will know how to look after himself?"

"Yes," said Hood gravely. "I've got a very fixed fundamental conviction that Crane will turn up again all right. But it's true that he may look jolly queer after going *fantee* for all that time."

It became a sort of pastime at the club of the Lunatics to compete in speculations about the guise in which the maddest of their madmen would return, after being so long lost to civilization. And grand preparations were made as for a sort of Walpurgis Night of nonsense when it was known at last that he was really returning. Hood had received letters from him occasionally, full of queer mythologies, and then a rapid succession of telegrams from places nearer and nearer home, culminating in the announcement that he would appear in the club that night. It was about five minutes before dinner-time that a sharp knock on the door announced his arrival.

"Bang all the gongs and the tom-toms," cried Wilding White. "The Lord High Mumbo-Jumbo arrives riding on the nightmare."

"We had better bring out the throne of the King of the Maniacs," said Hood, laughing. "We may want it at last," and he turned towards the big padded chair that still stood at the top of the table.

As he did so James Crane walked into the room. He was clad in very neat and well-cut evening clothes, not too fashionable, and a little formal. His hair was parted on one side, and his moustache clipped rather close; he took a seat with a pleasant smile, and began talking about the weather.

He was not allowed, however, to confine his conversation to the weather. He had certainly succeeded in giving his old friends the only sort of surprise that they really had not expected; but they were too old friends for their friend to be able to conceal from them the meaning of such a change. And it was on that festive evening that Crane explained his position; a position which he maintained in most things ever afterwards, and one which is the original foundation of the affair that follows.

"I have lived with the men we call savages all over the world," he said simply, "and I have found out one truth about them. And I tell you, my friends, you may talk about independence and individual self-expression till you burst. But I've always found, wherever I went, that the man who could really be trusted to keep his word, and to fight, and to work for his family, was the man who did a war-dance before the moon where the moon was worshipped, and wore a nose-ring in his nose where nose-rings were worn. I have had plenty of fun, and I won't interfere with anyone else having it. But I believe I have seen what is the real making of mankind, and I have come back to my tribe."

This was the first act of the drama which ended in the remarkable appearance and disappearance of Mr Enoch Oates, and it has been necessary to narrate it briefly before passing on to the second act. Ever since that time Crane had preserved at once his eccentric friends and his own more formal customs. And there were many among the newer members of the club who had never known him except as the Colonel, the grizzled, military gentleman whose severe scheme of black and white attire and strict politeness in small things formed the one foil of sharp contrast to that many-coloured Bohemia. One of these was Hilary Pierce, the young aviator; and much as he liked the Colonel, he never quite understood him. He had never known the old soldier in his volcanic youth, as had Hood and White, and therefore never knew how much of the fire remained under the rock or the snows. The singular affair of the hat, which has been narrated to the too patient reader elsewhere, surprised him more than it did the older men, who knew very well that the Colonel was not so old as he looked. And the impression increased with all the incidents which a fanatical love of truth has forced the chronicler to relate in the same connexion; the incident of the river and of the pigs and of the somewhat larger pet of Mr Wilding White. There was talk of renaming the Lunatic Asylum as the League of the Long Bow, and of commemorating its performances in a permanent ritual. The Colonel was induced to wear a crown of cabbage on state occasions, and Pierce was gravely invited to bring his pigs with him to dine at the club.

"You could easily bring a little pig in your large pocket," said Hood. "I often wonder people do not have pigs as pets."

"A pig in a poke, in fact," said Pierce. "Well, so long as you have the tact to avoid the indelicacy of having pork for dinner that evening, I suppose I could bring my pig in my pocket."

"White'd find it rather a nuisance to bring his elephant in his pocket," observed the Colonel.

Pierce glanced at him, and had again the feeling of incongruity at seeing the ceremonial cabbage adorning his comparatively venerable head. For the Colonel had just been married, and was rejuvenated in an almost jaunty degree. Somehow the philosophical young man seemed to miss something, and sighed. It was then that he made the remark which is the pivot of this precise though laborious anecdote.

"Since the Colonel ate his hat," he said, "the Lunatic Asylum has lacked a background."

"Damn your impudence," said the Colonel cheerfully. "Do you mean to call me a background to my face?"

"A dark background," said Pierce soothingly. "Do not resent my saying a dark background. I mean a grand, mysterious background like that of night; a sublime and even starry background."

"Starry yourself," said Crane indignantly.

"It was against that background of ancient night," went on the young man dreamily, "that the fantastic shapes and fiery colours of our carnival could really be seen. So long as he came here with his black coat and beautiful society manners there was a foil to our follies. We were eccentric, but he was our centre. You cannot be eccentric without a centre."

"I believe Hilary is quite right," said Owen Hood earnestly. "I believe we have made a great mistake. We ought not to have all gone mad at once. We ought to have taken it in turns to go mad. Then I could have been shocked at his behaviour on Mondays, Wednesdays, and Fridays, and he could have been shocked at my behaviour on Tuesdays, Thursdays, and Saturdays. But there is no moral value in going mad when nobody is shocked. If Crane leaves off being shocked, what are we to do?"

"I know what we want," began Pierce excitedly.

"So do I," interrupted Hood. "We want a sane man."

"Not so easy to find nowadays," said the old soldier. "Going to advertise?"

"I mean a stupid man," explained Owen Hood. "I mean a man who's conventional all through, not a humbug like Crane. I mean, I want a solid, serious, business man, a hard-headed, practical man of affairs, a man to whom vast commercial interests are committed. In a word, I want a fool; some beautiful, rounded, homogeneous fool, in whose blameless face, as in a round mirror, all our fancies may really be reflected and renewed. I want a very successful man, a very wealthy man, a man – "

"I know! I know!" cried young Pierce, almost waving his arms. "Enoch Oates!"

"Who's Enoch Oates?" inquired White.

"Are the lords of the world so little known?" asked Hood. "Enoch Oates is Pork, and nearly everything else; Enoch Oates is turning civilization into one vast sausage-machine. Didn't I ever tell you how Hilary ran into him over that pig affair?"

"He's the very man you want," cried Hilary Pierce enthusiastically. "I know him, and I believe I can get him. Being a millionaire, he's entirely ignorant. Being an American, he's entirely in earnest. He's got just that sort of negative Nonconformist conscience of New England that balances the positive money-getting of New York. If we want to surprise anybody we'll surprise him. Let's ask Enoch Oates to dinner."

"I won't have any practical jokes played on guests," said the Colonel.

"Of course not," replied Hood. "He'll be only too pleased to take it seriously. Did you ever know an American who didn't like seeing the Sights? And if you don't know you're a Sight with that cabbage on your head, it's time an American tourist taught you."

"Besides, there's a difference," said Pierce. "I wouldn't ask a fellow like that doctor, Horace Hunter – "

"Sir Horace Hunter," murmured Hood reverently.

"I wouldn't ask him, because I really think him a sneak and a snob, and my invitation could only be meant as an insult. But Oates is not a man I hate, nor is he hateful. That's the curious part of it. He's a simple, sincere sort of fellow, according to his lights, which are pretty dim. He's a thief and a robber of course, but he doesn't know it. I'm asking him because he's different; but I don't imagine he's at all sorry to be different. There's no harm in giving a man a good dinner and letting him be a background without knowing it."

When Mr Enoch Oates in due course accepted the invitation and presented himself at the club, many were reminded of that former occasion when a stiff and conventional figure in evening dress had first appeared like a rebuke to the revels. But in spite of the stiff sameness of both those black and white costumes, there was a great deal of difference between the old background and the new background. Crane's good manners were of that casual kind that are rather peculiarly English, and mark an aristocracy at its ease in the saddle. Curiously enough, if the American had one point in common with a Continental noble of ancient lineage (whom his daughter might have married any day), it was that they would both be a little more on the defensive, living in the midst of democracy. Mr Oates was perfectly polite, but there was something a little rigid about him. He walked to his chair rather stiffly and sat down rather heavily. He was a powerful, ponderous man with a large sallow face, a little suggestive of a corpulent Red Indian. He had a ruminant eye, and an equally ruminant manner of chewing an unlighted cigar. These were signs that might well have gone with a habit of silence. But they did not.

Mr Oates' conversation might not be brilliant, but it was continuous. Pierce and his friends had begun with some notion of dangling their own escapades before him, like dancing dolls before a child; they had told him something of the affair of the Colonel and his cabbage, of the captain and his pigs, of the parson and his elephant; but they soon found that their hearer had not come there merely as a listener. What he thought of their romantic buffooneries it would be hard to say; probably he did not understand them, possibly he did not even hear them. Anyhow, his own monologue went on. He was a leisurely speaker. They found themselves revising much that they had heard about the snap and smartness and hurry of American talk. He spoke without haste or embarrassment, his eye boring into space, and he more than fulfilled Mr Pierce's hopes of somebody who would talk about business matters. His talk was a mild torrent of facts and figures, especially figures. In fact the background was doing all it could to contribute the required undertone of common commercial life. The background was justifying all their hopes that it would be practical and prosaic. Only the background had rather the air of having become the foreground.

"When they put that up to me I saw it was the proposition," Mr Oates was saying. "I saw I'd got on to something better than my old regulation turnover of eighty-five thousand dollars on each branch. I reckoned I should save a hundred and twenty thousand dollars in the long run by scrapping the old plant, even if I had to drop another thirty thousand dollars on new works, where I'd get the raw material for a red cent. I saw right away that was the point to freeze on to; that I just got a chance to sell something I didn't need to buy; something that could be sort of given away like old match-ends. I figured out it would be better by a long chalk to let the other guys rear the stock and sell me their refuse for next to nix, so I could get ahead with turning it into the goods. So I started in right away and got there at the first go off with an increase of seven hundred and fifty-one thousand dollars."

"Seven hundred and fifty-one thousand dollars," murmured Owen Hood. "How soothing it all seems."

"I reckon those mutts didn't get on to what they were selling me," continued Mr Oates, "or didn't have the pep to use it that way themselves; for though it was the sure-enough hot tip, it isn't everybody would have thought of it. When I was in pork, of course, I wanted the other guys out; but just now I wasn't putting anything on pork, but only on just that part of a pig I wanted and they didn't want. By notifying all your pig farmers I was able to import nine hundred and twenty-five thousand pigs' ears this fall, and I guess I can get consignments all winter."

Hood had some little legal experience with long-winded commercial witnesses, and he was listening by this time with a cocked eyebrow and an attention much sharper than the dreamy ecstasy with which the poetic Pierce was listening to the millionaire's monologue, as if to the wordless music of some ever-murmuring brook.

"Excuse me," said Hood earnestly, "but did I understand you to say pigs' ears?"

"That is so, Mr Hood," said the American with great patience and politeness. "I don't know whether I gave you a sufficiently detailed description for you to catch on to the proposition, but – "

"Well," murmured Pierce wistfully, "it sounded to me like a detailed description."

"Pardon me," said Hood, checking him with a frown. "I really want to understand this proposition of Mr Oates. Do I understand that you bought pigs' ears cheap, when the pigs were cut up for other purposes, and that you thought you could use them for some purpose of your own?"

"Sure!" said Mr Enoch Oates, nodding. "And my purpose was about the biggest thing in fancy goods ever done in the States. In the publicity line there's nothing like saying you can do what folks say can't be done. Flying in the face of proverbs instead of providence, I reckon. It catches on at once. We got to work, and got out the first advertisement in no time; just a blank space with 'We Can Do It' in the middle. Got folks wondering for a week what it was."

"I hope, sir," said Pierce in a low voice, "that you will not carry sound commercial principles so far as to keep us wondering for a week what it was."

"Well," said Oates, "we found we could subject the pigskin and bristles to a new gelat'nous process for making artificial silk, and we figured that publicity would do the rest. We came out with the second set of posters: 'She Wants it Now'... 'The Most Wonderful Woman on Earth is waiting by the Old Fireside, hoping you'll bring her home a Pig's Whisper Purse.' "

"A purse!" gasped Hilary.

"I see you're on the notion," proceeded the unmoved American. "We called 'em Pig's Whisper Purses after the smartest and most popular poster we ever had: 'There was a Lady Loved a Swine.' You know the nursery rhyme, I guess; featured a slap-up princess whispering in a pig's ear. I tell you there isn't a smart woman in the States now that can do without one of our pig-silk purses, and all because it upsets the proverb. Why, see here – "

Hilary Pierce had sprung wildly to his feet with a sort of stagger and clutched at the American's arm.

"Found! Found!" he cried hysterically. "Oh, sir, I implore you to take the chair! Do, do take the chair!"

"Take the chair!" repeated the astonished millionaire, who was already almost struggling in his grasp. "Really, gentlemen, I hadn't supposed the proceedings were so formal as to require a chairman, but in any case – "

It could hardly be said, however, that the proceedings were formal. Mr Hilary Pierce had the appearance of forcibly dragging Mr Enoch Oates in the direction of the large padded armchair, that had always stood empty at the top of the club table, uttering cries which, though incoherent, appeared to be partly apologetic.

"No offence," he gasped. "Hope no misunderstanding...*Honoris causa*...you, you alone are worthy of that seat...the club has found its king and justified its title at last."

Here the Colonel intervened and restored order. Mr Oates departed in peace; but Mr Hilary Pierce was still simmering.

"And that is the end of our quiet, ordinary business man," he cried. "Such is the behaviour of our monochrome and unobtrusive background." His voice rose to a sort of wail. "And we thought we were dotty! We deluded ourselves with the hope that we were pretty well off our chump! Lord have mercy on us! American big business rises to a raving idiocy compared with which we are as sane as the beasts of the field. The modern commercial world is far madder than anything we can do to satirize it."

"Well," said the Colonel good-humouredly, "we've done some rather ridiculous things ourselves."

"Yes, yes," cried Pierce excitedly, "but we did them to make ourselves ridiculous. That unspeakable man is wholly, serenely serious. He thinks those maniacal monkey tricks are the normal life of man. Your argument really answers itself. We did the maddest things we could think of, meaning them to look mad. But they were nothing like so mad as what a modern business man does in the way of business."

"Perhaps it's the American business man," said White, "who's too keen to see the humour of it."

"Nonsense," said Crane. "Millions of Americans have a splendid sense of humour."

"Then how fortunate are we," said Pierce reverently, "through whose lives this rare, this ineffable, this divine being has passed."

"Passed away for ever, I suppose," said Hood with a sigh. "I fear the Colonel must be our only background once more."

Colonel Crane was frowning thoughtfully, and at the last words his frown deepened to disapproval. He puffed at his smouldering cigar and then, removing it, said abruptly:

"I suppose you fellows have forgotten how I came to be a background? I mean, why I rather approve of people being backgrounds."

"I remember something you said a long time ago," replied Hood. "Hilary must have been in long-clothes at that time."

"I said I had found out something by going round the world," said Crane. "You young people think I am an old Tory; but remember I am also an old traveller. Well, it's part of the same thing. I'm a traditionalist because I'm a traveller. I told you when I came back to the club that I'd come back to the tribe. I told you that in all the tribes of the world, the best man was the man true to his tribe. I told you the best man was the man who wore a nose-ring where nose-rings were worn."

"I remember," said Owen Hood.

"No, you forget," said Crane rather gruffly. "You forget it when you talk about Enoch Oates the American. I'm no politician, thank God, and I shall look on with detachment if you dynamite him for being a millionaire. As a matter of fact, he doesn't think half so much of money as old Normantowers, who thinks it's too sacred to talk about. But you're not dynamiting him for being a millionaire. You're simply laughing at him for being an American. You're laughing at him for being national and normal, for being a good citizen, a good tribesman, for wearing a nose-ring where nose-rings are worn."

"I say…Kuklux, you know," remonstrated Wilding White in his hazy way. "Americans wouldn't be flattered – "

"Do you suppose you haven't got a nose-ring?" cried Crane so sharply that the clergyman started from his trance and made a mechanical gesture as if to feel for that feature. "Do you suppose a man like you doesn't carry his nationality as plain as the nose on his face? Do you think a man as hopelessly English as you are wouldn't be laughed at in America? You can't be a good Englishman without being a good joke. The better Englishman you are the more of a joke you are; but still it's better to be better. Nose-rings are funny to people who don't wear 'em. Nations are funny to people who don't belong to 'em. But it's better to wear a nose-ring than to be a cosmopolitan crank who cuts off his nose to spite his face."

This being by far the longest speech the Colonel had ever delivered since the day he returned from his tropical travels long ago, his old friend looked at him with a certain curiosity; even his old friends hardly understood how much he had been roused in defence of a guest and of his own deep delicacies about the point of hospitality. He went on with undiminished warmth:

"Well, it's like that with poor Oates. He has, as we see it, certain disproportions, certain sensibilities, certain prejudices that stand out in our eyes like deformities. They offend you; they offend me, possibly rather more than they do you. You young revolutionists think you're very liberal and universal; but the only result is that you're narrow and national without knowing it. We old fogeys know our tastes are narrow and national; but we know they are only tastes. And we know, at any rate I know, that Oates is far more likely to be an honest man, a good husband and a good father, because he stinks of the rankest hickory patch in the Middle West, than if he were some fashionable New Yorker pretending to be an English aristocrat or playing the aesthete in Florence."

"Don't say a good husband," pleaded Pierce with a faint shudder. "It reminds me of the grand slap-up advertisement of the Pig's Whisper. How do you feel about that, my dear Colonel? The Most Wonderful Woman on Earth Waiting by the Old Fireside – "

"It makes my flesh creep," replied Crane. "It chills me to the spine. I feel I would rather die than have anything to do with it. But that has nothing to do with my point. I don't belong to the tribe who wear nose-rings; nor to the tribe who talk through their noses."

"Well, aren't you a little thankful for that?" asked White.

"I'm thankful I can be fair in spite of it," answered Crane. "When I put a cabbage on my head, I didn't expect people not to stare at it. And I know that each one of us in a foreign land is a foreigner, and a thing to be stared at."

"What I don't understand about him," said Hood, "is the sort of things he doesn't mind having stared at. How can people tolerate all that vulgar, reeking, gushing commercial cant everywhere? How can a man talk about the Old Fireside? It's obscene. The police ought to interfere."

"And that's just where you're wrong," said the Colonel. "It's vulgar enough and mad enough and obscene enough if you like. But it's not cant. I have travelled amongst these wild tribes, for years on end; and I tell you emphatically it is not cant. And if you want to know, just ask your extraordinary American friend about his own wife and his own relatively Old Fireside. He won't mind. That's the extraordinary part of it."

"What does all this really mean, Colonel?" asked Hilary Pierce.

"It means, my boy," answered the Colonel, "that I think you owe our guest an apology."

So it came about that there was an epilogue, as there had been a prologue, to the drama of the entrance and exit of Mr Enoch B Oates; an epilogue which in its turn became a prologue to the later dramas of the League of the Long Bow. For the words of the Colonel had a certain influence on the Captain, and the actions of the Captain had a certain influence on the American millionaire; and so the whole machinery of events was started afresh by that last movement over the nuts and wine, when Colonel Crane had stirred moodily in his seat and taken his cigar out of his mouth.

Hilary Pierce was an amiable and even excessively optimistic young man by temperament, in spite of his pugnacity; he would really have been the last man in the world to wish to hurt the feelings of a harmless stranger; and he had a deep and almost secret respect for the opinions of the older soldier. So, finding himself soon afterwards passing the great gilded gateways of the highly American hotel that was the London residence of the American, he paused a moment in hesitation and then went in and gave his name to various overpowering officials in uniforms that might have been those of the German General Staff. He was relieved when the large American came out to meet him with a simple and lumbering affability, and offered his large limp hand as if there had never been a shadow of misunderstanding. It was somehow borne in upon Pierce that his own rather intoxicated behaviour that evening had merely been noted down along with the architectural styles and the mellow medievalism of the pig-sty, as part of the fantasies of a feudal land. All the antics of the Lunatic Asylum had left the American traveller with the impression that similar parlour games were probably being played that evening in all the parlours of England. Perhaps there was something, after all, in Crane's suggestion that every nation assumes that every other nation is a sort of mild madhouse.

Mr Enoch Oates received his guest with great hospitality and pressed on him cocktails of various occult names and strange colours, though he himself partook of nothing but a regimen of tepid milk.

Pierce fell into the confidence of Mr Enoch Oates with a silent swiftness that made his brain reel with bewilderment. He was staggered like a man who had fallen suddenly through fifteen floors of a skyscraper and found himself in somebody's bedroom. At the lightest hint of the sort of thing to which Colonel Crane had alluded, the American opened himself with an expansiveness that was like some gigantic embrace. All the interminable tables of figures and calculations in dollars had for the moment disappeared; yet Oates was talking in the same easy and natural nasal drawl, very leisurely and a little monotonous, as he said:

"I'm married to the best and brightest woman God ever made, and I tell you it's her and God between them that have made me, and I reckon she had the hardest part of it. We had nothing but a few sticks when I started; and it was the way she stood by that gave me the heart to risk even those on my own judgement of how things were going in the Street. I counted on a rise in Pork, and if it hadn't risen I'd have been broke and I dare say in the jug. But she's just wonderful. You should see her."

He produced her photograph with a paralysing promptitude; it represented a very regal lady dressed up to the nines, probably for the occasion, with very brilliant eyes and an elaborate load of light hair.

" 'I believe in your star, Enoch,' she said; 'you stick to Pork,' " said Oates, with tender reminiscence, "and so we saw it through."

Pierce, who had been speculating with involuntary irreverence on the extreme difficulty of conducting a love affair or a sentimental conversation in which one party had to address the other as Enoch, felt quite ashamed of his cynicism when the Star of Pork shone with such radiance in the eyes of his new friend.

"It was a terrible time, but I stuck to Pork, sometimes feeling she could see clearer than I could; and of course she was right, and I've never known her wrong. Then came my great chance of making the combination and freezing out competition; and I was able to give her the sort of things she ought to have and let her take the lead as she should. I don't care for society much myself; but I'm often glad on a late night at the office to ring her up and hear she's enjoying it."

He spoke with a ponderous simplicity that seemed to disarm and crush the criticism of a more subtle civilization. It was one of those things that are easily seen to be absurd; but even after they are seen to be absurd, they are still there. It may be, after all, that that is the definition of the great things.

"I reckon that's what people mean by the romance of business," continued Oates, "and though my business got bigger and bigger, it made me feel kinda pleased there had been a romance at the heart of it. It had to get bigger, because we wanted to make the combination watertight all over the world. I guess I had to fix things up a bit with your politicians. But Congress men are alike all the world over, and it didn't trouble me any."

There was a not uncommon conviction among those acquainted with Captain Hilary Pierce that that ingenious young man was cracked. He did a great many things to justify the impression; and in one sense certainly had never shown any reluctance to make a fool of himself. But if he was a lunatic, he was none the less a very English lunatic. And the notion of talking about his most intimate affections, suddenly, to a foreigner in a hotel, merely because the conversation had taken that turn, was something that he found quite terrifying. And yet an instinct, an impulse running through all these developments, told him that a moment had come and that he must seize some opportunity that he hardly understood.

"Look here," he said rather awkwardly, "I want to tell you something."

He looked down at the table as he continued.

"You said just now you were married to the best woman in the world. Well, curiously enough, so am I. It's a coincidence that often happens. But it's a still more curious coincidence that, in our own quiet way, we went in for Pork too. She kept pigs at the back of the little country inn where I met her; and at one time it looked as if the pigs might have to be given up. Perhaps the inn as well. Perhaps the wedding as well. We were quite poor, as poor as you were when you started; and to the poor those extra modes of livelihood are often life. We might have been ruined; and the reason was, I gather, that you had gone in for Pork. But after all ours was the real pork; pork that walked about on legs. We made the bed for the pigs and filled the inside of the pig; you only bought and sold the name of the pig. You didn't go to business with a live little pig under your arm or walk down Wall Street followed by a herd of swine. It was a phantom pig, the ghost of a pig, that was able to kill our real pig and perhaps us as well. Can you really justify the way in which your romance nearly ruined our romance? Don't you think there must be something wrong somewhere?"

"Well," said Oates after a very long silence, "that's a mighty big question and will take a lot of discussing."

But the end to which their discussion led must be left to reveal itself when the prostrate reader has recovered sufficient strength to support the story of The Unthinkable Theory of Professor Green, which those who would endure to the end may read at some later date.

VI

The Unthinkable Theory of Professor Green

If the present passage in the chronicles of the Long Bow seem but a side issue, an interlude and an idyll, a mere romantic episode lacking that larger structural achievement which gives solidity and hard actuality to the other stories, the reader is requested not to be hasty in his condemnation; for in the little love story of Mr Oliver Green is to be found, as in a parable, the beginning of the final apotheosis and last judgement of all these things.

It may well begin on a morning when the sunlight came late but brilliant, under the lifting of great clouds from a great grey sweep of wolds that grew purple as they dipped again into distance. Much of that mighty slope was striped and scored with ploughed fields, but a rude path ran across it, along which two figures could be seen in full stride outlined against the morning sky.

They were both tall; but beyond the fact that they had both once been professional soldiers, of rather different types and times, they had very little in common. By their ages they might almost have been father and son; and this would not have been contradicted by the fact that the younger appeared to be talking all the time, in a high, confident and almost crowing voice, while the elder only now and then put in a word. But they were not father and son; strangely enough they were really talking and walking together because they were friends. Those who know only too well their proceedings as narrated elsewhere would have recognized Colonel Crane, once of the Coldstream Guards, and Captain Pierce, late of the Flying Corps.

The young man appeared to be talking triumphantly about a great American capitalist whom he professed to have persuaded to see the error of his ways. He talked rather as if he had been slumming.

"I'm very proud of it, I can tell you," he said. "Anybody can produce a penitent murderer. It's something to produce a penitent millionaire. And I do believe that poor Enoch Oates has seen the light (thanks to my conversations at lunch); since I talked to him, Oates is another and a better man."

"Sown his wild oats, in fact," remarked Crane.

"Well," replied the other. "In a sense they were very quiet oats. Almost what you might call Quaker Oats. He was a Puritan and a Prohibitionist and a Pacifist and an Internationalist; in short, everything that is in darkness and the shadow of death. But what you said about him was quite right. His heart's in the right place. It's on his sleeve. That's why I preached the gospel to the noble savage and made him a convert."

"But what did you convert him to?" inquired the other.

"Private property," replied Pierce promptly. "Being a millionaire he had never heard of it. But when I explained the first elementary idea of it in a simple form, he was quite taken with the notion. I pointed out that he might abandon robbery on a large scale and create property on a small scale. He felt it was very revolutionary, but he admitted it was right. Well, you know, he'd bought this big English estate out here. He was going to play the philanthropist, and have a model estate with all the regular trimmings; heads hygienically shaved by machinery every morning; and the cottagers admitted once a month into their own front gardens and told to keep off the grass. But I said to him: 'If you're going to give things to people, why not give 'em? If you give your friend a plant in a pot, you don't send him an inspector from the Society for the Prevention of Cruelty to Vegetables to see he waters it properly. If you give your friend a box of cigars, you don't make him write a monthly report of how many he smokes a day. Can't you be a little generous with your generosity? Why don't you use your money to make free men instead of to make slaves? Why don't you give your tenants their land and have done with it, or let 'em have it very cheap?' And he's done it; he's really done it. He's created hundreds of small proprietors, and changed the whole of this countryside. That's why I want you to come up and see one of the small farms."

"Yes," said Colonel Crane, "I should like to see the farm."

"There's a lot of fuss about it, too; there's the devil of a row," went on the young man, in very high spirits. "Lots of big combines and things are trying to crush the small farmers with all sorts of tricks; they even complain of interference by an American. You can imagine how much Rosenbaum Low and Goldstein and Guggenheimer must be distressed by the notion of a foreigner interfering in England. I want to know how a foreigner could interfere less than by giving back their land to the English people and clearing out. They all put it on to me; and right they are. I regard Oates as my property; my convert; captive of my bow and spear."

"Captive of your long bow I imagine," said the Colonel. "I bet you told him a good many things that nobody but a shrewd business man would have been innocent enough to believe."

"If I use the long bow," replied Pierce with dignity, "it is a weapon with heroic memories proper to a yeoman of England. With what more fitting weapon could we try to establish a yeomanry?"

"There is something over there," said Crane quietly, "that looks to me rather like another sort of weapon."

They had by this time come in full sight of the farm buildings which crowned the long slope; and beyond a kitchen garden and an orchard rose a thatched roof with a row of old-fashioned lattice windows under it; the window at the end standing open. And out of this window at the edge of the block of buildings protruded a big black object, rigid and apparently cylindrical, thrust out above the garden and dark against the morning daylight.

"A gun!" cried Pierce involuntarily; "looks just like a howitzer; or is it an anti-aircraft gun?"

"Anti-airman gun, no doubt," said Crane; "they heard you were coming down and took precautions."

"But what the devil can he want with a gun?" muttered Pierce, peering at the dark outline.

"And who the devil is *he*, if it comes to that?" said the Colonel.

"Why, that window," explained Pierce, "that's the window of the room they've let to a paying guest, I know. Man of the name of Green, I understand; rather a recluse, and I suppose some sort of crank."

"Not an anti-armament crank, anyhow" said the Colonel.

"By George!" said Pierce, whistling softly. "I wonder whether things really have moved faster than we could fancy! I wonder whether it's a revolution or a civil war beginning after all. I suppose we are an army ourselves; I represent the Air Force and you represent the infantry."

"You represent the infants," answered the Colonel. "You're too young for this world; you and your revolutions! As a matter of fact, it isn't a gun, though it does look rather like one. I see now what it is."

"And what in the world is it?" asked his friend.

"It's a telescope," said Crane. "One of those very big telescopes they usually have in observatories."

"Couldn't be partly a gun and partly a telescope?" pleaded Pierce, reluctant to abandon his first fancy. "I've often seen the phrase 'shooting stars,' but perhaps I've got the grammar and sense of it wrong. The young man lodging with the farmer may be following one of the local sports – the local substitute for duck-shooting!"

"What in the world are you talking about?" growled the other.

"Their lodger may be shooting the stars," explained Pierce.

"Hope their lodger isn't shooting the moon," said the flippant Crane.

As they spoke there came towards them, through the green and twinkling twilight of the orchard, a young woman with copper-coloured hair and a square and rather striking face, whom Pierce saluted respectfully as the daughter of the house. He was very punctilious upon the point that these new peasant farmers must be treated like small squires and not like tenants or serfs.

"I see your friend Mr Green has got his telescope out," he said.

"Yes, sir," said the girl. "They say Mr Green is a great astronomer."

"I doubt if you ought to call me 'sir,' " said Pierce reflectively. "It suggests rather the forgotten feudalism than the new equality. Perhaps you might oblige me by saying 'Yes, citizen,' then we could continue our talk about Citizen Green on an equal footing. By the way, pardon me, let me present Citizen Crane."

Citizen Crane bowed politely to the young woman without any apparent enthusiasm for his new title; but Pierce went on:

"Rather rum to call ourselves citizens when we're all so glad to be out of the city. We really want some term suitable to rural equality. The Socialists have spoilt 'Comrade'; you can't be a comrade without a Liberty tie and a pointed beard. Morris had a good notion of one man calling another Neighbour. That sounds a little more rustic. I suppose," he added wistfully to the girl, "I suppose I could not induce you to call me Gaffer?"

"Unless I'm mistaken," observed Crane, "that's your astronomer wandering about in the garden. Thinks he's a botanist, perhaps. Appropriate to the name of Green."

"Oh, he often wanders in the garden and down to the meadow and the cowsheds," said the young woman. "He talks to himself a good deal, explaining a great theory he's got. He explains it to everybody he meets, too. Sometimes he explains it to me when I'm milking the cow."

"Perhaps you can explain it to us?" said Pierce.

"Not so bad as that," she said, laughing. "It's something like that Fourth Dimension they talk about. But I've no doubt he'll explain it to you if you meet him."

"Not for me," said Pierce. "I'm a simple peasant proprietor and ask nothing but Three Dimensions and a Cow."

"Cow's the Fourth Dimension, I suppose," said Crane.

"I must go and attend to the Fourth Dimension," she said with a smile.

"Peasants all live by patchwork, running two or three side-shows," observed Pierce. "Curious sort of livestock on the farm. Think of people living on a cow and chickens and an astronomer."

As he spoke the astronomer approached along the path by which the girl had just passed. His eyes were covered with huge horn spectacles of a dim blue colour; for he was warned to save his eyesight for his starry vigils. This gave a misleading look of morbidity to a face that was naturally frank and healthy; and the figure, though stooping, was stalwart. He was very absent-minded. Every now and then he looked at the ground and frowned as if he did not like it.

Oliver Green was a very young professor, but a very old young man. He had passed from science as the hobby of a schoolboy to science as the ambition of a middle-aged man, without any intermediate holiday of youth. Moreover, his monomania had been fixed and frozen by success; at least by a considerable success for a man of his years. He was already a fellow of the chief learned societies connected with his subject, when there grew up in his mind the grand, universal, all-sufficing Theory which had come to fill the whole of his life as the daylight fills the day. If we attempted the exposition of that theory here, it is doubtful whether the result would resemble daylight. Professor Green was always ready to prove it; but if we were to set out the proof in this place, the next four or five pages would be covered with closely printed columns of figures, brightened here and there by geometrical designs, such as seldom form part of the text of a romantic story. Suffice it to say that the theory had something to do with Relativity and the reversal of the relations between the stationary and the moving object. Pierce, the aviator, who had passed much of his time on moving objects not without the occasional anticipation of bumping into stationary objects, talked to Green a little on the subject. Being interested in scientific aviation, he was nearer to the abstract sciences than were his friends, Crane with his hobby of folklore or Hood with his love of classic literature or Wilding White with his reading of the mystics. But the young aviator frankly admitted that Professor Green soared high into the heavens of the Higher Mathematics, far beyond the flight of his little aeroplane.

The Professor had begun, as he always began, by saying that it was quite easy to explain; which was doubtless true, as he was always explaining it. But he often ended by affirming fallaciously that it was quite easy to understand, and it would be an exaggeration to say that it was always understood. Anyhow, he was just about to read his great paper on his great theory at the great Astronomical Congress that was to be held that year at Bath; which was one reason why he had pitched his astronomical camp, or emplaced his astronomical gun, in the house of Farmer Dale on the hills of Somerset. Mr Enoch Oates could not but feel the lingering hesitation of the landlord when he heard that his protégés the Dales were about to admit an unknown stranger into their household. But Pierce sternly reminded him that this paternal attitude was a thing of the past and that a free peasant was free to let lodgings to a homicidal maniac if he liked. Nevertheless, Pierce was rather relieved to find the maniac was only an astronomer; but it would have been all the same if he had been an astrologer. Before coming to the farm, the astronomer had set up his telescope in much dingier places – in lodgings in Bloomsbury and the grimy buildings of a Midland University. He thought he was, and to a great extent he was, indifferent to his surroundings. But for all that the air and colour of those country surroundings were slowly and strangely sinking into him.

"The idea is simplicity itself," he said earnestly, when Pierce rallied him about the theory. "It is only the proof that is, of course, a trifle technical. Put in a very crude and popular shape, it depends on the mathematical formula for the inversion of the sphere."

"What we call turning the world upside down," said Pierce. "I'm all in favour of it."

"Everyone knows the idea of relativity applied to motion," went on the Professor. "When you run out of a village in a motor car, you might say that the village runs away from you."

"The village does run away when Pierce is out motoring," remarked Crane. "Anyhow, the villagers do. But he generally prefers to frighten them with an aeroplane."

"Indeed?" said the astronomer with some interest. "An aeroplane would make an even better working model. Compare the movement of an aeroplane with what we call merely for convenience the fixity of the fixed stars."

"I dare say they got a bit unfixed when Pierce bumped into them," said the Colonel.

Professor Green sighed in a sad but patient spirit. He could not help being a little disappointed even with the most intelligent outsiders with whom he conversed. Their remarks were pointed but hardly to the point. He felt more and more that he really preferred those who made no remarks. The flowers and the trees made no remarks; they stood in rows and allowed him to lecture to them for hours on the fallacies of accepted astronomy. The cow made no remarks. The girl who milked the cow made no remarks; or, if she did, they were pleasant and kindly remarks, not intended to be clever. He drifted, as he had done many times before, in the direction of the cow.

The young woman who milked the cow was not in the common connotation what is meant by a milkmaid. Margery Dale was the daughter of a substantial farmer already respected in that county. She had been to school and learnt various polite things before she came back to the farm and continued to do the thousand things that she could have taught the schoolmasters. And something of this proportion or disproportion of knowledge was dawning on Professor Green, as he stood staring at the cow and talking, often in a sort of soliloquy. For he had a rather similar sensation of a great many other things growing up thickly like a jungle round his own particular thing; impressions and implications from all the girl's easy actions and varied avocations. Perhaps he began to have a dim suspicion that he was the schoolmaster who was being taught.

The earth and the sky were already beginning to be enriched with evening; the blue was already almost a glow like apple-green behind the line of branching apple trees; against it the bulk of the farm stood in a darker outline, and for the first time he realized something quaint or queer added to that outline by his own big telescope stuck up like a gun pointed at the moon. Somehow it looked, he could not tell why, like the beginning of a story. The hollyhocks also looked incredibly tall. To see what he would have called "flowers" so tall as that seemed like seeing a daisy or a dandelion as large as a lamp-post. He was positive there was nothing exactly like it in Bloomsbury. These tall flowers also looked like the beginning of a story – the story of Jack and the Beanstalk. Though he knew little enough of what influences were slowly sinking into him, he felt something apt in the last memory. Whatever was moving within him was something very far back, something that came before reading and writing. He had some dream, as from a previous life, of dark streaks of field under stormy clouds of summer and the sense that the flowers to be found there were things like gems. He was in that country home that every cockney child feels he has always had and never visited.

"I have to read my paper tonight," he said abruptly. "I really ought to be thinking about it."

"I do hope it will be a success," said the girl; "but I rather thought you were always thinking about it."

"Well, I was – generally," he said in a rather dazed fashion; and indeed it was probably the first time that he had ever found himself fully conscious of not thinking about it. Of what he was thinking about he was by no means fully conscious.

"I suppose you have to be awfully clever even to understand it," observed Margery Dale conversationally.

"I don't know," he said, slightly stirred to the defensive. "I'm sure I could make you see – I don't mean you aren't clever, of course; I mean I'm quite sure you're clever enough to see – to see anything."

"Only some sorts of things, I'm afraid," she said, smiling. "I'm sure your theory has got nothing to do with cows and milking-stools."

"It's got to do with anything," he said eagerly; "with everything, in fact. It would be just as easy to prove it from stools and cows as anything else. It's really quite simple. Reversing the usual mathematical formula, it's possible to reach the same results in reality by treating motion as a fixed point and stability as a form of motion. You were told that the earth goes round the sun, and the moon goes round the earth. Well, in my formula, we first treat it as if the sun went round the earth – "

She looked up radiantly. "I always *thought* it looked like that," she said emphatically.

"And you will, of course, see for yourself," he continued triumphantly, "that by the same logical inversion we must suppose the earth to be going round the moon."

The radiant face showed a shadow of doubt and she said "Oh!"

"But any of the things you mention, the milking-stool or the cow or what not, would serve the same purpose, since they are objects generally regarded as stationary."

He looked up vaguely at the moon which was steadily brightening as vast shadows spread over the sky.

"Well, take those things you talk of," he went on, moved by a meaningless unrest and tremor. "You see the moon rise behind the woods over there and sweep in a great curve through the sky and seem to set again beyond the hill. But it would be just as easy to preserve the same mathematical relations by regarding the moon as the centre of the circle and the curve described by some object such as the cow – "

She threw her head back and looked at him, with eyes blazing with laughter that was not in any way mockery but a childish delight at the crowning coincidence of a fairy-tale.

"Splendid!" she cried. "So the cow really does jump over the moon!"

Green put up his hand to his hair; and after a short silence said suddenly like a man recalling a recondite Greek quotation:

"Why I've heard that somewhere. There was something else – 'The little dog laughed – ' "

Then something happened, which was in the world of ideas much more dramatic than the fact that the little dog laughed. The professor of astronomy laughed. If the world of things had corresponded to the world of ideas, the leaves of the apple tree might have curled up in fear or the birds dropped out of the sky. It was rather as if the cow had laughed.

Following on that curt and uncouth noise was a silence; and then the hand he had raised to his head abruptly rent off his big blue spectacles and showed his staring blue eyes. He looked boyish and even babyish.

"I wondered whether you always wore them," she said. "I should think they made that moon of yours look blue. Isn't there a proverb or something about a thing happening once in a blue moon?"

He threw the great goggles on the ground and broke them.

"Good gracious!" she exclaimed, "you seem to have taken quite a dislike to them all of a sudden. I thought you were going to wear them till – well, till all is blue, as they say."

He shook his head. "All is beautiful," he said. "You are beautiful."

The young woman was normally very lucid and decisive in dealing with gentlemen who made remarks of that kind, especially when she concluded that the gentlemen were not gentlemen. But for some reason in this case it never occurred to her that she needed defence; possibly because the other party seemed more defenceless than indefensible. She said nothing. But the other party said a great deal, and his remarks did not grow more rational. At that moment, far away in their inn-parlour in the neighbouring town, Hood and Crane and the fellowship of the Long Bow were actually discussing with considerable interest the meaning and possibilities of the new astronomical theory. In Bath the lecture hall was being prepared for the exposition of the theory. The theorist had forgotten all about it.

"I have been thinking a good deal," Hilary Pierce was saying, "about that astronomical fellow who is going to lecture in Bath tonight. It seemed to me somehow that he was a kindred spirit and that sooner or later we were bound to get mixed up with him – or he was bound to get mixed up with us. I don't say it's always very comfortable to get mixed up with us. I feel in my bones that there is going to be a big row soon. I feel as if I'd consulted an astrologer; as if Green were the Merlin of our Round Table. Anyhow, the astrologer has an interesting astronomical theory."

"Why?" inquired Wilding White with some surprise. "What have you got to do with his theory?"

"Because," answered the young man, "I understand his astronomical theory a good deal better than he thinks I do. And, let me tell you, his astronomical theory is an astronomical allegory."

"An allegory?" repeated Crane. "What of?"

"An allegory of us," said Pierce; "and, as with many an allegory, we've acted it without knowing it. I realized something about our history, when he was talking, that I don't think I'd ever thought of before."

"What in the world are you talking about?" demanded the Colonel.

"His theory," said Pierce in a meditative manner, "has got something to do with moving objects being really stationary, and stationary objects being really moving. Well, you always talk of me as if I were a moving object."

"Heartbreaking object sometimes," assented the Colonel with cordial encouragement.

"I mean," continued Pierce calmly, "that you talk of me as if I were always motoring too fast or flying too far. And what you say of me is pretty much what most people say of you. Most sane people think we all go a jolly lot too far. They think we're a lot of lunatics outrunning the constable or looping the loop, and always up to some new nonsense. But when you come to think of it, it's we who always stay where we are, and the rest of the world that's always moving and shifting and changing."

"Yes," said Owen Hood; "I begin to have some dim idea of what you are talking about."

"In all our little adventures," went on the other, "we have all of us taken up some definite position and stuck to it, however difficult it might be; that was the whole fun of it. But our critics did not stick to their own position – not even to their own conventional or conservative position. In each one of the stories it was they who were fickle, and we who were fixed. When the Colonel said he would eat his hat, he did it; when he found it meant wearing a preposterous hat, he wore it. But his neighbours didn't even stick to their own conviction that the hat was preposterous. Fashion is too fluctuating and sensitive a thing; and before the end, half of them were wondering whether they oughtn't to have hats of the same sort. In that affair of the Thames factory, Hood admired the old landscape and Hunter admired the old landlords. But Hunter didn't go on admiring the old landlords; he deserted to the new landlords as soon as they got the land. His conservatism was too snobbish to conserve anything. I wanted to import pigs, and I went on importing pigs, though my methods of smuggling might land me in a madhouse. But Enoch Oates, the millionaire, didn't go on importing pork; he went off at once on some new stunt, first on the booming of his purses, and afterwards on the admirable stunt of starting English farms. The business mind isn't steadfast; even when it can be turned the right way, it's too easy to turn. And everything has been like that, down to the little botheration about the elephant. The police began to prosecute Mr White, but they soon dropped it when Hood showed them that he had some backing. Don't you see that's the moral of the whole thing? The modern world is materialistic, but it isn't solid. It isn't hard or stern or ruthless in pursuit of its purpose, or all the things that the newspapers and novels say it is; and sometimes actually praise it for being. Materialism isn't like stone; it's like mud, and liquid mud at that."

"There's something in what you say," said Owen Hood, "and I should be inclined to add something to it. On a rough reckoning of the chances in modern England, I should say the situation is something like this. In that dubious and wavering atmosphere it is very unlikely there would ever be a revolution, or any very vital reform. But if there were, I believe on my soul that it might be successful. I believe everything else would be too weak and wobbly to stand up against it."

"I suppose that means," said the Colonel, "that you're going to do something silly."

"Silliest thing I can think of," replied Pierce cheerfully. "I'm going to an astronomical lecture."

The degree of silliness involved in the experiment can be most compactly and clearly stated in the newspaper report, at which the friends of the experimentalists found themselves gazing with more than their usual bewilderment on the following morning. The Colonel, sitting at his club with his favourite daily paper spread out before him, was regarding with a grave wonder a paragraph that began with the following headlines:

"AMAZING SCENE AT SCIENTIFIC CONGRESS

"LECTURER GOES MAD AND ESCAPES

"A scene equally distressing and astonishing took place at the third meeting of the Astronomical Society now holding its congress at Bath. Professor Oliver Green, one of the most promising of the younger astronomers, was set down in the syllabus to deliver a lecture on 'Relativity in Relation to Planetary Motion.' About an hour before the lecture, however, the authorities received a telegram from Professor Green, altering the subject of his address on the ground that he had just discovered a new star, and wished immediately to communicate his discovery to the scientific world. Great excitement and keen anticipation prevailed at the meeting, but these feelings changed to bewilderment as the lecture proceeded. The lecturer announced without hesitation the existence of a new planet attached to one of the fixed stars, but proceeded to describe its geological formation and other features with a fantastic exactitude beyond anything yet obtained by way of the spectrum or the telescope. He was understood to say that it produced life in an extravagant form, in towering objects which constantly doubled or divided themselves until they ended in flat filaments, or tongues of a bright green colour. He was proceeding to give a still more improbable description of a more mobile but equally monstrous form of life, resting on four trunks or columns which swung in rotation, and terminating in some curious curved appendages, when a young man in the front row, whose demeanour had shown an increasing levity, called out abruptly: 'Why, that's a cow!' To this the professor, abandoning abruptly all pretence of scientific dignity, replied by shouting in a voice like thunder: 'Yes, of course it's a cow; and you fellows would never have noticed a cow, even if she jumped over the moon!' The unfortunate professor then began to rave in the most incoherent manner, throwing his arms about and shouting aloud that he and his fellow scientists were all a pack of noodles who had never looked at the world they were walking on, which contained the most miraculous things. But the latter part of his remarks, which appeared to be an entirely irrelevant outburst in praise of the beauty of Woman, were interrupted by the Chairman and officials of the Congress, who called for medical and constabulary interference. No less a person than Sir Horace Hunter, who, although best known as a psycho-physiologist, has taken all knowledge for his province and was present to show his interest in astronomical progress, was able to certify on the spot that the unfortunate Green was clearly suffering from dementia, which was immediately corroborated by a local doctor, so that the unhappy man might be removed without further scandal.

"At this point, however, a still more extraordinary development took place. The young man in the front row, who had several times interrupted the proceedings with irrelevant remarks, sprang to his feet, and loudly declaring that Professor Green was the only sane man in the Congress, rushed at the group surrounding him, violently hurled Sir Horace Hunter from the platform, and with the assistance of a friend and fellow-rioter, managed to recapture the lunatic from the doctors and police, and carry him outside the building. Those pursuing the fugitives found themselves at first confronted with a new mystery in the form of their complete disappearance. It has since been discovered that they actually escaped by aeroplane; the young man, whose name is said to be Pierce, being a well-known aviator formerly connected with the Flying Corps. The other young man, who assisted him and acted as pilot, has not yet been identified."

Night closed and the stars stood out over Dale's Farm; and the telescope pointed at the stars in vain. Its giant lenses had vainly mirrored the moon of which its owner had spoken in so vain a fashion; but its owner did not return. Miss Dale was rather unaccountably troubled by his absence, and mentioned it once or twice; after all, as her family said, it was very natural that he should go to an hotel in Bath for the night, especially if the revels of the roystering astronomers were long and late. "It's no affair of ours," said the farmer's wife cheerfully. "He is not a child." But the farmer's daughter was not quite so sure on the point.

Next morning she rose even earlier than usual and went about her ordinary tasks, which by some accident or other seemed to look more ordinary than usual. In the blank morning hours, it was perhaps natural that her mind should go back to the previous afternoon, when the conduct of the astronomer could by no means be dismissed as ordinary.

"It's all very well to say he's not a child," she said to herself. "I wish I were as certain he's not an idiot. If he goes to an hotel, they'll cheat him."

The more angular and prosaic her own surroundings seemed in the daylight, the more doubt she felt about the probable fate of the moonstruck gentleman who looked at a blue moon through his blue spectacles. She wondered whether his family or his friends were generally responsible for his movements; for really he must be a little dotty. She had never heard him talk about his family; and she remembered a good many things he had talked about. She had never even seen him talking to a friend, except once to Captain Pierce, when they talked about astronomy. But the name of Captain Pierce linked itself up rapidly with other and more relevant suggestions. Captain Pierce lived at the Blue Boar on the other side of the down, having been married a year or two before to the daughter of the innkeeper, who was an old friend of the daughter of the farmer. They had been to the same school in the neighbouring provincial town, and had once been, as the phrase goes, inseparable. Perhaps friends ought to pass through the phase in which they are inseparable to reach the phase in which they can safely be separated.

"Joan might know something about it," she said to herself. "At least her husband might know."

She turned back into the kitchen and began to rout things out for breakfast; when she had done everything she could think of doing for a family that had not yet put in an appearance, she went out again into the garden and found herself at the same gate, staring at the steep wooded hill that lay between the farm and the valley of the Blue Boar. She thought of harnessing the pony; and then went walking rather restlessly along the road over the hill.

On the map it was only a few miles to the Blue Boar; and she was easily capable of walking ten times the distance. But maps, like many other scientific documents, are very inaccurate. The ridge that ran between the two valleys was, relatively to that rolling plain, as definite as a range of mountains. The path through the dark wood that lay just beyond the farm began like a lane and then seemed to go up like a ladder. By the time she had scaled it, under its continuous canopy of low spreading trees, she had the sensation of having walked for a long time. And when the ascent ended with a gap in the trees and a blank space of sky, she looked over the edge like one looking into another world.

Mr Enoch Oates, in his more expansive moments, had been known to allude to what he called God's Great Prairies. Mr Rosenbaum Low, having come to London from, or through, Johannesburg, often referred in his imperialistic speeches to the "illimitable veldt." But neither the American prairie nor the African veldt really looks any larger, or could look any larger, than a wide English vale seen from a low English hill. Nothing can be more distant than the distance; the horizon or the line drawn by heaven across the vision of man. Nothing is so illimitable as that limit. Within our narrow island there is a whole series of such infinities; as if the island itself could contain seven seas. As she looked out over that new landscape, the soul seemed to be slaked and satisfied with immensity and, by a paradox, to be filled at last with emptiness. All things seemed not only great but growing in greatness. She could fancy that the tall trees standing up in the sunlight grew taller while she looked at them. The sun was rising and it seemed as if the whole world rose with it. Even the dome of heaven seemed to be lifting slowly; as if the very sky were a skirt drawn up and disappearing into the altitudes of light.

The vast hollow below her was coloured as variously as a map in an atlas. Fields of grass or grain or red earth seemed so far away that they might have been the empires and kingdoms of a world newly created. But she could already see on the brow of a hill above the pine-woods the pale scar of the quarry and below it the glittering twist in the river where stood the inn of the Blue Boar. As she drew nearer and nearer to it she could see more and more clearly a green triangular field with tiny black dots, which were little black pigs; and another smaller dot, which was a child. Something like a wind behind her or within her, that had driven her over the hills, seemed to sweep all the long lines of that landslide of a landscape, so that they pointed to that spot.

As the path dropped to the level and she began to walk by farms and villages, the storm in her mind began to settle and she recovered the reasonable prudence with which she had pottered about her own farm. She even felt some responsibility and embarrassment about troubling her friend by coming on so vague an errand. But she told herself convincingly enough that after all she was justified. One would not normally be alarmed about a strayed lodger as if he were a lion escaped from a menagerie. But she had after all very good reason for regarding this lion as rather a fearful wildfowl. His way of talking had been so eccentric that everybody for miles round would have agreed, if they had heard him, that he had a tile loose. She was very glad they had not heard him; but their imaginary opinion fortified her own. They had a duty in common humanity; they could not let a poor gentleman of doubtful sanity disappear without further inquiry.

She entered the inn with a firm step and hailed her friend with something of that hearty cheerfulness that is so unpopular in the early riser. She was rather younger and by nature rather more exuberant than Joan; and Joan had already felt the drag and concentration of children. But Joan had not lost her rather steely sense of humour, and she heard the main facts of her friend's difficulty with a vigilant smile.

"We should rather like to know what has happened," said the visitor with vague carelessness. "If anything unpleasant had happened, people might even blame us, when we knew he was like that."

"Like what?" asked Joan smiling.

"Why, a bit off, I suppose we must say," answered the other. "The things he said to me about cows and trees and having found a new star were really – "

"Well, it's rather lucky you came to me," said Joan quietly. "For I don't believe you'd have found anybody else on the whole face of the earth who knows exactly where he is now."

"And where is he?"

"Well, he's not on the face of the earth," said Joan Hardy.

"You don't mean he's – dead?" asked the other in an unnatural voice.

"I mean he's up in the air," said Joan, "or, what is often much the same thing, he is with my husband. Hilary rescued him when they were just going to nab him, and carried him off in an aeroplane. He says they'd better hide in the clouds for a bit. You know the way he talks; of course, they do come down every now and then when it's safe."

"Escaped! Nabbed him! Safe!" ejaculated the other young woman with round eyes. "What in the world does it all mean?"

"Well," replied her friend, "he seems to have said the same sort of things that he said to you to a whole roomful of scientific men at Bath. And, of course, the scientific men all said he was mad; I suppose that's what scientific men are for. So they were just going to take him away to an asylum, when Hilary – "

The farmer's daughter rose in a glory of rage that might have seemed to lift the roof, as the great sunrise had seemed to lift the sky.

"Take him away!" she cried. "How dare they talk about such things? How dare they say he is mad? It's they who must be mad to say such stuff! Why, he's got more brains in his boots than they have in all their silly old bald heads knocked together – and I'd like to knock 'em together! Why, they'd all smash like eggshells, and he's got a head like cast iron. Don't you know he's beaten all the old duffers at their own business, of stars and things? I expect they're all jealous; it's just what I should have expected of them."

The fact that she was entirely unacquainted with the names, and possibly the existence, of these natural philosophers did not arrest the vigorous word-painting with which she completed their portraits. "Nasty spiteful old men with whiskers," she said, "all bunched together like so many spiders and weaving dirty cobwebs to catch their betters; of course, it's all a conspiracy. Just because they're all mad and hate anybody who's quite sane."

"So you think he's quite sane?" asked her hostess gravely.

"Sane? What do you mean? Of course he's quite sane," retorted Margery Dale.

With a mountainous magnanimity Joan was silent. Then after a pause she said:

"Well, Hilary has taken his case in hand and your friend's safe for the present; Hilary generally brings things off, however queer they sound. And I don't mind telling you in confidence that he's bringing that and a good many other things off, rather big things, just now. You can't keep him from fighting whatever you do; and he seems to be out just now to fight everybody. So I shouldn't wonder if you saw all your old gentlemen's heads knocked together after all. There are rather big preparations going on; that friend of his named Blair is for ever going and coming with his balloons and things; and I believe something will happen soon on a pretty large scale, perhaps all over England."

"Will it?" asked Miss Dale in an absent-minded manner (for she was sadly deficient in civic and political sense). "Is that your Tommy out there?"

And they talked about the child and then about a hundred entirely trivial things; for they understood each other perfectly.

And if there are still things the reader fails to understand, if (as seems almost incredible) there are things that he wishes to understand, then it can only be at the heavy price of studying the story of The Unprecedented Architecture of Commander Blair; and with that, it is comforting to know, the story of all these things will be drawing near its explanation and its end.

VII

The Unprecedented Architecture of Commander Blair

The Earl of Eden had become Prime Minister for the third time, and his face and figure were therefore familiar in the political cartoons and even in the public streets. His yellow hair and lean and springy figure gave him a factitious air of youth; but his face on closer study looked lined and wrinkled and gave almost a shock of decrepitude. He was in truth a man of great experience and dexterity in his own profession. He had just succeeded in routing the Socialist Party and overthrowing the Socialist Government, largely by the use of certain rhymed mottoes and maxims which he had himself invented with considerable amusement. His great slogan of "Don't Nationalize but Rationalize" was generally believed to have led him to victory. But at the moment when this story begins he had other things to think of. He had just received an urgent request for a consultation from three of his most prominent supporters – Lord Normantowers, Sir Horace Hunter, OBE, the great advocate of scientific politics, and Mr R Low, the philanthropist. They were confronted with a problem, and their problem concerned the sudden madness of an American millionaire.

The Prime Minister was not unacquainted with American millionaires, even those whose conduct suggested that they were hardly representative of a normal or national type. There was the great Grigg, the millionaire inventor, who had pressed upon the War Office a scheme for finishing the War at a blow; it consisted of electrocuting the Kaiser by wireless telegraphy There was Mr Napper, of Nebraska, whose negotiations for removing Shakespeare's Cliff to America as a symbol of Anglo-Saxon unity were unaccountably frustrated by the firm refusal of the American Republic to send us Plymouth Rock in exchange. And there was that charming and cultured Bostonian, Colonel Hoopoe, whom all England welcomed in his crusade for Purity and the League of the Lily until England discovered with considerable surprise that the American Ambassador and all respectable Americans flatly refused to meet the Colonel, whose record at home was that of a very narrow escape from Sing-Sing.

But the problem of Enoch Oates, who had made his money in pork, was something profoundly different. As Lord Eden's three supporters eagerly explained to him, seated round a garden table at his beautiful country seat in Somerset, Mr Oates had done something that the maddest millionaire had never thought of doing before. Up to a certain point he had proceeded in a manner normal to such a foreigner. He had purchased amid general approval an estate covering about a quarter of a county; and it was expected that he would make it a field for some of those American experiments in temperance or eugenics for which the English agricultural populace offer a sort of virgin soil. Instead of that, he suddenly went mad and made a present of his land to his tenants; so that by an unprecedented anomaly the farms became the property of the farmers. That an American millionaire should take away English things from England, English rent, English relics, English pictures, English cathedrals or cliffs of Dover, was a natural operation to which everybody was by this time accustomed. But that an American millionaire should give English land to English people was an unwarrantable interference and tantamount to an alien enemy stirring up revolution. Enoch Oates had therefore been summoned to the Council, and sat scowling at the table as if he were in the dock.

"Results most deplorable already," said Sir Horace Hunter, in his rather loud voice. "Give you an example, my lord; people of the name of Dale in Somerset took in a lunatic as a lodger. May have been a homicidal maniac for all I know; some do say he had a great cannon or culverin sticking out of his bedroom window. But with no responsible management of the estate, no landlord, no lawyer, no educated person anywhere, there was nothing to prevent their letting the bedroom to a Bengal tiger. Anyhow, the man was mad, rushed raving on to the platform at the Astronomical Congress talking about Lovely Woman and the cow that jumped over the moon. That damned agitator Pierce, who used to be in the Flying Corps, was in the hall, and made a riot and carried the crazy fellow off in an aeroplane. That's the sort of thing you'll have happening all over the place if these ignorant fellows are allowed to do just as they like."

"It is quite true," said Lord Normantowers. "I could give many other examples. They say that Owen Hood, another of these eccentrics, has actually bought one of these little farms and stuck it all round with absurd battlements and a moat and drawbridge, with the motto 'The Englishman's House is his Castle.'"

"I think," said the Prime Minister quietly, "that however English the Englishman may be, he will find his castle is a castle in Spain; not to say a castle in the air. Mr Oates," he said, addressing very courteously the big brooding American at the other end of the table, "please do not imagine that I cannot sympathize with such romances, although they are only in the air. But I think in all sincerity that you will find they are unsuited to the English climate. *Et ego in Arcadia,* you know; we have all had such dreams of all men piping in Arcady. But after all, you have already paid the piper; and if you are wise, I think you can still call the tune."

"Gives me great gratification to say it's too late," growled Oates. "I want them to learn to play and pay for themselves."

"But you want them to learn," said Lord Eden gently, "and I should not be in too much of a hurry to call it too late. It seems to me that the door is still open for a reasonable compromise; I understand that the deed of gift, considered as a legal instrument, is still the subject of some legal discussion and may well be subject to revision. I happened to be talking of it yesterday with the law officers of the Crown; and I am sure that the least hint that you yourself– "

"I take it to mean," said Mr Oates with great deliberation, "that you'll tell your lawyers it'll pay them to pick a hole in the deal."

"That is what we call the bluff Western humour," said Lord Eden, smiling, "but I only mean that we do a great deal in this country by reconsideration and revision. We make mistakes and unmake them. We have a phrase for it in our history books; we call it the flexibility of an unwritten constitution."

"We have a phrase for it too," said the American reflectively. "We call it graft."

"Really" cried Normantowers, a little bristly man, with sudden shrillness, "I did not know you were so scrupulous in your own methods."

"Motht unthcrupulouth," said Mr Low virtuously

Enoch Oates rose slowly like an enormous leviathan rising to the surface of the sea; his large sallow face had never changed in expression; but he had the air of one drifting dreamily away.

"Wal," he said, "I dare say it's true I've done some graft in my time, and a good many deals that weren't what you might call modelled on the Sermon on the Mount. But if I smashed people, it was when they were all out to smash me; and if some of 'em were poor, they were the sort that were ready to shoot or knife or blow me to bits. And I tell you, in my country the whole lot of you would be lynched or tarred and feathered tomorrow, if you talked about lawyers taking away people's land when once they'd got it. Maybe the English climate's different, as you say; but I'm going to see it through. As for you, Mr Rosenbaum – "

"My name is Low," said the philanthropist. "I cannot thee why anyone should object to uthing my name."

"Not on your life," said Mr Oates affably. "Seems to be a pretty appropriate name."

He drifted heavily from the room, and the four other men were left, staring at a riddle.

"He's going on with it, or, rather, they're going on with it," groaned Horace Hunter. "And what the devil is to be done now?"

"It really looks as if he were right in calling it too late," said Lord Normantowers bitterly. "I can't think of anything to be done."

"I can," said the Prime Minister. They all looked at him; but none of them could read the indecipherable subtleties in his old and wrinkled face under his youthful yellow hair.

"The resources of civilization are not exhausted," he said grimly. "That's what the old governments used to say when they started shooting people. Well, I could understand you gentlemen feeling inclined to shoot people now. I suppose it seems to you that all your power in the State, which you wield with such public spirit of course, all Sir Horace's health reforms, the Normantowers' new estate, and so on, are all broken to bits, to rotten little bits of rusticity. What's to become of a governing class if it doesn't hold all the land, eh? Well, I'll tell you. I know the next move, and the time has come to take it."

"But what is it?" demanded Sir Horace.

"The time has come," said the Prime Minister, "to Nationalize the Land."

Sir Horace Hunter rose from his chair, opened his mouth, shut it, and sat down again, all with what he himself might have called a reflex action.

"But that is Socialism!" cried Lord Normantowers, his eyes standing out of his head.

"True Socialism, don't you think?" mused the Prime Minister. "Better call it True Socialism; just the sort of thing to be remembered at elections. Theirs is Socialism, and ours is True Socialism."

"Do you really mean, my lord," cried Hunter in a heat of sincerity stronger than the snobbery of a lifetime, "that you are going to support the Bolshies?"

"No," said Eden, with the smile of a sphinx. "I mean the Bolshies are going to support me. Idiots!"

After a silence, he added in a more wistful tone:

"Of course, as a matter of sentiment, it is a little sad. All our fine old English castles and manors, the homes of the gentry...they will become public property, like post offices, I suppose. When I think of the happy hours I have myself passed at Normantowers – " He smiled across at the nobleman of that name and went on. "And Sir Horace has now, I believe, the joy of living in Warbridge Castle – fine old place. Dear me, yes, and I think Mr Low has a castle, though the name escapes me."

"Rosewood Castle," said Mr Low rather sulkily.

"But I say," cried Sir Horace, rising, "what becomes of 'Don't Nationalize but Rationalize'?"

"I suppose," replied Eden lightly, "it will have to be 'Don't Rationalize but Nationalize.' It comes to the same thing. Besides, we can easily get a new motto of some sort. For instance, we, after all, are the patriotic party, the national party. What about 'Let the Nationalists Nationalize'?"

"Well, all I can say is – " began Normantowers explosively.

"Compensation, there will be compensation, of course," said the Prime Minister soothingly; "a great deal can be done with compensation. If you will all turn up here this day week, say at four o'clock, I think I can lay all the plans before you."

When they did turn up next week and were shown again into the Prime Minister's sunny garden, they found that the plans were, indeed, laid before them; for the table that stood on the sunny lawn was covered with large and small maps and a mass of official documents. Mr Eustace Pym, one of the Prime Minister's numerous private secretaries, was hovering over them, and the Prime Minister himself was sitting at the head of the table studying one of them with an intelligent frown.

"I thought you'd like to hear the terms of the arrangements," he said. "I'm afraid we must all make sacrifices in the cause of progress."

"Oh, progress be – " cried Normantowers, losing patience. "I want to know if you really mean that my estate – "

"It comes under the department of Castle and Abbey Estates in Section Four," said Lord Eden, referring to the paper before him. "By the provisions of the new Bill the public control in such cases will be vested in the Lord-Lieutenant of the County. In the particular case of your castle – let me see – why, yes, of course, you are Lord Lieutenant of that county."

Little Lord Normantowers was staring, with his stiff hair all standing on end; but a new look was dawning in his shrewd though small-featured face.

"The case of Warbridge Castle is different," said the Prime Minister. "It happens unfortunately to stand in a district desolated by all the recent troubles about swine-fever, touching which the Health Controller" (here he bowed to Sir Horace Hunter) "has shown such admirable activity. It has been necessary to place the whole of this district in the hands of the Health Controller, that he may study any traces of swinefever that may be found in the Castle, the Cathedral, the Vicarage, and so on. So much for that case, which stands somewhat apart; the others are mostly normal. Rosenbaum Castle – I should say Rosewood Castle – being of a later date, comes under Section

Five, and the appointment of a permanent Castle Custodian is left to the discretion of the Government. In this case the Government has decided to appoint Mr Rosewood Low to the post, in recognition of his local services to social science and economics. In all these cases, of course, due compensation will be paid to the present owners of the estates, and ample salaries and expenses of entertainment paid to the new officials, that the places maybe kept up in a manner worthy of their historical and national character."

He paused, as if for cheers, and Sir Horace was vaguely irritated into saying: "But look here, my castle – "

"Damn it all!" said the Prime Minister, with his first flash of impatience and sincerity. "Can't you see you'll get twice as much as before? First you'll be compensated for losing your castle, and then you'll be paid for keeping it."

"My lord," said Lord Normantowers humbly, "I apologize for anything I may have said or suggested. I ought to have known I stood in the presence of a great English statesman."

"Oh, it's easy enough," said Lord Eden frankly. "Look how easily we remained in the saddle, in spite of democratic elections; how we managed to dominate the Commons as well as the Lords. It'll be the same with what they call Socialism. We shall still be there; only we shall be called bureaucrats instead of aristocrats."

"I see it all now!" cried Hunter, "and by Heaven, it'll be the end of all this confounded demagogy of Three Acres and a Cow."

"I think so," said the Prime Minister with a smile; and began to fold up the maps.

As he was folding up the last and largest, he suddenly stopped and said:

"Hallo!"

A letter was lying in the middle of the table; a letter in a sealed envelope, and one which he evidently did not recognize as any part of his paper paraphernalia.

"Where did this letter come from?" he asked rather sharply. "Did you put it here, Eustace?"

"No," said Mr Pym staring. "I never saw it before. It didn't come with your letters this morning."

"It didn't come by post at all," said Lord Eden; "and none of the servants brought it in. How the devil did it get out here in the garden?"

He ripped it open with his finger and remained for some time staring in mystification at its contents.

> "Welkin Castle, Sept. 4th, 19— .
>
> "Dear Lord Eden, – As I understand you are making public provision for the future disposal of our historic national castles, such as Warbridge Castle, I should much appreciate any information about your intentions touching Welkin Castle, my own estate, as it would enable me to make my own arrangements. – Yours very truly,
>
> "Welkyn of Welkin."

"Who is Welkyn?" asked the puzzled politician; "he writes as if he knew me; but I can't recall him at the moment. And where is Welkin Castle? We must look at the maps again."

But though they looked at the maps for hours, and searched Burke, Debrett, "Who's Who," the atlas, and every other work of reference, they could come upon no trace of that firm but polite country gentleman.

Lord Eden was a little worried, because he knew that curiously important people could exist in a corner in this country, and suddenly emerge from their corner to make trouble. He knew it was very important that his own governing class should stand with him in this great public change (and private understanding), and that no rich eccentric should be left out or offended. But although he was worried to that extent, it is probable that his worry would soon have faded from his mind if it had not been for something that happened some days later.

Going out into the same garden to the same table, with the more agreeable purpose of taking tea there, he was amazed to find another letter, though this was lying not on the table but on the turf just beside it. It was unstamped like the other and addressed in the same handwriting; but its tone was more stern.

> "Welkin Castle, Oct. 6th, 19— .
>
> "My Lord, – As you seem to have decided to continue your sweeping scheme of confiscation, as in the case of Warbridge Castle, without the slightest reference to the historic and even heroic claims and traditions of Welkin Castle, I can only inform you that I shall defend the fortress of my fathers to the death. Moreover, I have decided to make a protest of a more public kind; and when you next hear from me it will be in the form of a general appeal to the justice of the English people. –
>
> Yours truly
>
> "Welkyn of Welkin."

The historic and even heroic traditions of Welkin Castle kept a dozen of the Prime Minister's private secretaries busy for a week, looking up encyclopedias and chronicles and books of history. But the Prime Minister himself was more worried about another problem. How did these mysterious letters get into the house, or rather into the garden? None of them came by post and none of the servants knew anything about them. Moreover, the Prime Minister, in an unobtrusive way, was very carefully guarded. Prime Ministers always are. But he had been especially protected ever since the Vegetarians a few years before had gone about killing everybody who believed in killing animals. There were always plain-clothes policemen at every entrance of his house and garden. And from their testimony it would appear certain that the letter could not have got into the garden; but for the trifling fact that it was lying there on the garden table. Lord Eden cogitated in a grim fashion for some time; then he said as he rose from his chair:

"I think I will have a talk to our American friend Mr Oates."

Whether from a sense of humour or a sense of justice, Lord Eden summoned Enoch Oates before the same special jury of three; or summoned them before him, as the case may be. For it was even more difficult than before to read the exact secret of Eden's sympathies or intentions; he talked about a variety of indifferent subjects leading up to that of the letters, which he treated very lightly. Then he said quite suddenly:

"Do you know anything about those letters, by the way?"

The American presented his poker face to the company for some time without reply. Then he said:

"And what makes you think I know anything about them?"

"Because," said Horace Hunter, breaking in with uncontrollable warmth, "we know you're hand and glove with all those lunatics in the League of the Long Bow who are kicking up all this shindy."

"Well," said Oates calmly, "I'll never deny I like some of their ways. I like live wires myself; and, after all, they're about the liveliest thing in this old country. And I'll tell you more. I like people who take trouble; and, believe me, they do take trouble. You say they're all nuts; but I reckon there really is method in their madness. They take trouble to keep those crazy vows of theirs. You spoke about the fellows who carried off the astronomer in an aeroplane. Well, I know Bellew Blair, the man who worked with Pierce in that stunt, and believe me he's not a man to be sniffed at. He's one of the first experts in aeronautics in the country; and if he's gone over to them, it means there's something in their notion for a scientific intellect to take hold of. It was Blair that worked that pig stunt for Hilary Pierce; made a great gas-bag shaped like a sow and gave all the little pigs parachutes."

"Well, there you are," cried Hunter. "Of all the lunacy – "

"I remember Commander Blair in the War," said the Prime Minister quietly. "Bellows Blair, they called him. He did expert work: some new scheme with dirigible balloons. But I was only going to ask Mr Oates whether he happens to know where Welkin Castle is."

"Must be somewhere near here," suggested Normantowers, "as the letters seem to come by hand."

"Well, I don't know," said Enoch Oates doubtfully. "I know a man living in Ely who had one of those letters delivered by hand. And I know another near Land's End who thought the letter must have come from somebody living near. As you say, they all seem to come by hand."

"By what hand?" asked the Prime Minister, with a queer, grim expression.

"Mr Oates," said Lord Normantowers firmly, "where is Welkin Castle?"

"Why it's everywhere, in a manner of speaking," said Mr Oates reflectively. "It's anywhere, anyhow. Gee – !" he broke off suddenly: "Why, as a matter of fact, it's here!"

"Ah," said the Prime Minister quietly, "I thought we should see something if we watched here long enough! You didn't think I kept you hanging about here only to ask Mr Oates questions that I knew the answer to."

"What do you mean? Thought we would see what?"

"Where the unstamped letters come from," replied Lord Eden.

Luminous and enormous, there heaved up above the garden trees something that looked at first like a coloured cloud; it was flushed with light such as lies on clouds opposite the sunset, a light at once warm and wan; and it shone like an opaque flame. But as it came closer it grew more and more incredible. It took on solid proportions and perspective, as if a cloud could brush and crush the dark tree-tops. It was something never seen before in the sky; it was a cubist cloud. Men gazing at such a sunset cloud-land often imagine they see castles and cities of an almost uncanny completeness. But there would be a possible point of completeness at which they would cry aloud, or perhaps shriek aloud, as at a sign in heaven; and that completeness had come. The big luminous object that sailed above the garden was outlined in battlements and turrets like a fairy castle; but with an architectural exactitude impossible in any cloud-land. With the very look of it a phrase and a proverb leapt into the mind.

"There, my lord!" cried Oates, suddenly lifting his nasal and drawling voice and pointing, "there's that dream you told me about. There's your castle in the air."

As the shadow of the flying thing travelled over the sunlit lawn, they looked up and saw for the first time that the lower part of the edifice hung downwards like the car of a great balloon. They remembered the aeronautical tricks of Commander Blair and Captain Pierce and the model of the monstrous pig. As it passed over the table a white speck detached itself and dropped from the car. It was a letter.

The next moment the white speck was followed by a shower that was like a snowstorm. Countless letters, leaflets, and scraps of paper were littered all over the lawn. The guests seemed to stand staring wildly in a wilderness of waste-paper; but the keen and experienced eyes of Lord Eden recognized the material which, in political elections, is somewhat satirically called "literature."

It took the twelve private secretaries some time to pick them all up and make the lawn neat and tidy again. On examination they proved to be mainly of two kinds: one a sort of electioneering pamphlet of the League of the Long Bow, and the other a somewhat airy fantasy about private property in air. The most important of the documents, which Lord Eden studied more attentively, though with a grim smile, began with the sentence in large letters:

"An Englishman's House Is No Longer His Castle On The Soil Of England. If It Is To Be His Castle, It Must Be A Castle In The Air.

"If There Seem To Be Something Unfamiliar And Even Fanciful In The Idea, We Reply That It Is Not Half So Fantastic To Own Your Own Houses In The Clouds As Not To Own Your Own Houses On The Earth."

Then followed a passage of somewhat less solid political value, in which the acute reader might trace the influence of the poetical Mr Pierce rather than the scientific Mr Blair. It began "They Have Stolen the Earth; We Will Divide the Sky." But the writer followed this with a somewhat unconvincing claim to have trained rooks and swallows to hover in rows in the air to represent the hedges of "the blue meadows of the new realm," and he was so obliging as to accompany the explanation with diagrams of space showing the exact ornithological boundaries in dotted lines. There were other equally scientific documents dealing with the treatment of clouds, the driving of birds to graze on insects, and so on. The whole of this section concluded with the great social and economic slogan: "Three Acres and a Crow."

But when Lord Eden read on, his attention appeared graver than this particular sort of social reconstruction would seem to warrant. The writer of the pamphlet resumed:

"Do not be surprised if there seems to be something topsy-turvy in the above programme. That topsy-turvydom marks the whole of our politics. It may seem strange that the air which has always been public should become private, when the land which has always been private has become public. We answer that this is exactly how things really stand today in the matter of all publicity and privacy. Private things are indeed being made public. But public things are being kept private.

"Thus we all had the pleasure of seeing in the papers a picture of Sir Horace Hunter, OBE, smiling in an ingratiating manner at his favourite cockatoo. We know this detail of his existence, which might seem a merely domestic one. But the fact that he is shortly to be paid thirty thousand pounds of public money, for continuing to live in his own house, is concealed with the utmost delicacy.

"Similarly we have seen whole pages of an illustrated paper filled with glimpses of Lord Normantowers enjoying his honeymoon, which the papers in question are careful to describe as his Romance. Whatever it may be, an antiquated and fastidious taste might possibly be disposed to regard it as his own affair. But the fact that the taxpayer's money which is the taxpayer's affair, is to be given him in enormous quantities, first for going out of his castle, and then for coming back into it – this little domestic detail is thought too trivial for the taxpayer to be told of it.

"Or again, we are frequently informed that the hobby of Mr Rosenbaum Low is improving the breed of Pekinese, and God knows they need it. But it would seem the sort of hobby that anybody might have without telling everybody else about it. On the other hand, the fact that Mr Rosenbaum Low is being paid twice over for the same house, and keeping the house as well, is concealed from the public; along with the equally interesting fact that he is allowed to do these things chiefly because he lends money to the Prime Minister."

The Prime Minister smiled still more grimly and glanced in a light yet lingering fashion at some of the accompanying leaflets. They seemed to be in the form of electioneering leaflets, though not apparently connected with any particular election.

"Vote for Crane. He Said He would Eat His Hat and Did It. Lord Normantowers said he would explain how people came to swallow his coronet; but he hasn't done it yet.

"Vote for Pierce. He Said Pigs Would Fly And They Did. Rosenbaum Low said a service of international aerial express trains would fly; and they didn't. It was your money he made to fly.

"Vote for the League of the Long Bow. They Are The Only Men Who Don't Tell Lies."

The Prime Minister stood gazing after the vanishing cloud-castle, as it faded into the clouds, with a curious expression in his eyes. Whether it were better or worse for his soul, there was something in him that understood much that the muddled materialists around him could never understand.

"Quite poetical, isn't it?" he said dryly. "Wasn't it Victor Hugo or some French poet who said something about politics and the clouds?... The people say, 'Bah, the poet is in the clouds.' So is the thunderbolt."

"Thunderbolts!" said Normantowers contemptuously. "What can these fools do but go about flinging fireworks?"

"Quite so," replied Eden; "but I'm afraid by this time they are flinging fireworks into a powder-magazine."

He continued to gaze into the sky with screwed-up eyes, though the object had become invisible.

If his eye could really have followed the thing after which he gazed, he would have been surprised; if his unfathomable scepticism was still capable of surprise. It passed over woods and meadows like a sunset cloud towards the sunset, or a little to the north-west of it, like the fairy castle that was west of the moon. It left behind the green orchards and the red towers of Hereford and passed into bare places whose towers are mightier than any made by man, where they buttress the mighty wall of Wales. Far away in this wilderness of columned cliffs and clefts it found a cleft or hollow, along the floor of which ran a dark line that might have been a black river running through a rocky valley. But it was in fact a crack opening below into another abyss. The strange flying-ship followed the course of the winding fissure till it came to a place where the crack opened into a chasm, round like a cauldron and accidental as the knot in some colossal tree-trunk; through which it sank, entering the twilight of the tremendous cavern beneath. The abyss below was lit here and there with artificial lights, like fallen stars of the underworld, and bridged with wooden platforms and galleries, on which were wooden huts and huge packing-cases and many things somewhat suggestive of a munition dump. On the rocky walls were spread out various balloon coverings, some of them of even more grotesque outline than the castle. Some were in the shapes of animals; and on that primeval background looked like the last fossils, or possibly the first outlines of vast prehistoric creatures. Perhaps there was something suggestive in the fancy that in that underworld a new world was being created. The man who alighted from the flying castle recognized, almost as one recognizes a domestic pet, the outline of a highly primitive pig stretching like a large archaic drawing across the wall. For the young man was called Hilary Pierce, and had had previous dealings with the flying pig, though for that day he had been put in charge of the flying castle.

On the platform on which he alighted stood a table covered with papers, with almost more papers than Lord Eden's table. But these papers were covered almost entirely with figures and numbers and mathematical symbols. Two men were bending over the table, discussing and occasionally disputing. In the taller of the two the scientific world might have recognized Professor Green, whom it was seeking everywhere like the Missing Link, to incarcerate him in the interests of science. In the shorter and sturdier figure a very few people might have recognized Bellew Blair, the organizing brain of the English Revolution.

"I haven't come to stay," explained Pierce hastily. "I'm going on in a minute."

"Why shouldn't you stay?" asked Blair, in the act of lighting a pipe.

"I don't want your talk interrupted. Still less, far, far less, do I want it uninterrupted. I mean while I'm here. A little of your scientific conversation goes a long way with me; I know what you're like when you're really chatty. Professor Green will say in his satirical way '9920.05,' to which you will reply with quiet humour '75.007.' This will be too good an opening for a witty fellow like the Professor, who will instantly retort '982.09.' Not in the best taste perhaps, but a great temptation in the heat of debate."

"Commander Blair," said the Professor, "is very kind to let me share his calculations."

"Lucky for me," said Blair. "I'd have done ten times more with a mathematician like you."

"Well," said Pierce casually, "as you are so much immersed in mathematics, I'll leave you. As a matter of fact, I had a message for Professor Green, about Miss Dale at the house where he was lodging; but we mustn't interrupt scientific studies for a little thing like that."

Green's head came up from the papers with great abruptness.

"Message!" he cried eagerly. "What message? Is it really for me?"

"8282.003," replied Pierce coldly.

"Don't be offended," said Blair. "Give the Professor his message and then go if you like."

"It's only that she came over to see my wife to find out where you had gone to," said Pierce. "I told her, so far as it's possible to tell anybody. That's all," he added, but rather with the air of one saying "it ought to be enough."

Apparently it was, for Green, who was once more looking down upon the precious papers, crumpled one of them in his clenched hand unconsciously, like a man suddenly controlling his feelings.

"Well, I'm off" said Pierce cheerfully; "got to visit the other dumps."

"Stop a minute," said Blair, as the other turned away. "Haven't you any sort of public news as well as private news? How are things going in the political world?"

"Expressed in mathematical formula," replied Pierce over his shoulder, "the political news is MP squared plus LSD over U equals L. L let loose. L upon earth, my boy."

And he climbed again into his castle of the air.

Oliver Green stood staring at the crumpled paper and suddenly began to straighten it out.

"Mr Blair," he said, "I am terribly ashamed of myself. When I see you living here like a hermit in the mountains and scrawling your calculations, so to speak, on the rocks of the wilderness, devoted to your great abstract idea, vowed to a great cause, it makes me feel very small to have entangled you and your friends in my small affairs. Of course, the affair isn't at all small to me; but it must seem very small to you."

"I don't know very precisely" answered Blair, "what was the nature of the affair. But that is emphatically your affair. For the rest, I assure you we're delighted to have you, apart from your valuable services as a calculating machine."

Bellew Blair, the last and, in the worldly sense, by far the ablest of the recruits of the Long Bow, was a man in early middle age, square built, but neat in figure and light on his feet, clad in a suit of leather. He mostly moved about so quickly that his figure made more impression than his face; but when he sat down smoking, in one of his rare moments of leisure, as now, it could be remarked that his face was rather calm than vivacious; a short square face with a short resolute nose, but reflective eyes much lighter than his close black hair.

"It's quite Homeric," he added, "the two armies fighting for the body of an astronomer. You would be a sort of symbol anyhow, since they started that insanity of calling you insane. Nobody has any business to bother you about the personal side of the matter."

Green seemed to be ruminating, and the last phrase awoke him to a decision. He began to talk. Quite straightforwardly, though with a certain schoolboy awkwardness, he proceeded to tell his friend the whole of his uncouth love-story – the overturning of his spiritual world to the tune the old cow died of, or rather danced to.

"And I've let you in for hiding me like a murderer," he concluded. "For the sake of something that must seem to you, not even like a cow jumping over the moon, but more like a calf falling over the milking-stool. Perhaps people vowed to a great work like this ought to leave all that sort of thing behind them."

"Well, I don't see anything to be ashamed of," said Blair, "and in this case I don't agree with what you say about leaving those things behind. Of some sorts of work it's true; but not this. Shall I tell you a secret?"

"If you don't mind."

"The cow never does jump over the moon," said Blair gravely. "It's one of the sports of the bulls of the herd."

"I'm afraid I don't know what you mean," said the Professor.

"I mean that women can't be kept out of this war, because it's a land war," answered Blair. "If it were really a war in the air, you could have done it all by yourself. But in all wars of peasants defending their farms and homes, women have been very much on the spot; as they used to pour hot water out of windows during the Irish evictions. Look here, I'll tell you a story. It's relevant because it has a moral. After all, it's my turn, so to speak. You've told me the true story of the Cow that Jumped over the Moon. It's time I told you the true story of the Castle in the Air."

He smoked silently for a moment, and then said:

"You may have wondered how a very prosaic practical Scotch engineer like myself ever came to make a thing like that pantomime palace over there, as childish as a child's coloured balloon. Well, the answer is the same; because in certain circumstances a man may be very different from himself. At a certain period of the old war preparations, I was doing some work for the government in a secluded part of the western coast of Ireland. There were very few people for me to talk to; but one of them was the daughter of a bankrupt squire named Malone; and I talked to her a good deal. I was about as mechanical a mechanic as you could dig out anywhere; grimy, grumpy, tinkering about with dirty machinery. She was really like those princesses you read about in the Celtic poems; with a red crown made of curling elf-locks like little flames, and a pale elfin face that seemed somehow thin and luminous like glass; and she could make you listen to silence like a song. It wasn't a pose with her, it was a poem; there are people like that, but very few of them like her. I tried to keep my end up by telling her about the wonders of science, and the great new architecture of the air. And then Sheila used to say, 'And what is the good of them to me, when you *have* built them. I can see a castle build itself without hands out of gigantic rocks of clear jewels in the sky every night.' And she would point to where crimson or violet clouds hung in the green after-glow over the great Atlantic.

"You would probably say I was mad, if you didn't happen to have been mad yourself. But I was wild with the idea that there was something she admired and that she thought science couldn't do. I was as morbid as a boy; I half thought she despised me; and I wanted half to prove her wrong and half to do whatever she thought right. I resolved my science should beat the clouds at their own game; and I laboured till I'd actually made a sort of rainbow castle that would ride on the air. I think at the back of my mind there was some sort of crazy idea of carrying her off into the clouds she lived among, as if she were literally an angel and ought to dwell on wings. It never quite came to that, as you will hear, but as my experiments progressed my romance progressed too. You won't need any telling about that; I only want to tell you the end of the story because of the moral. We made arrangements to get married; and I had to leave a good many of the arrangements to her, while I completed my great work. Then at last it was ready and I came to seek her like a pagan god descending in a cloud to carry a nymph up to Olympus. And I found she had already taken a very solid little brick villa on the edge of a town, having got it remarkably cheap and furnished it with most modern conveniences. And when I talked to her about castles in the air, she laughed and said her castle had come down to the ground. That is the moral. A woman, especially an Irishwoman, is always uncommonly practical when it comes to getting married. That is what I meant by saying it is never the cow who jumps over the moon. It is the cow who stands firmly planted in the middle of the three acres; and who always counts in any struggle of the land. That is why there must be women in this story especially like those in your story and Pierce's, women who come from the land. When the world needs a Crusade for communal ideals, it is best waged by men without ties, like the Franciscans. But when it comes to a fight for private property – you can't keep women out of that. You can't have the family farm without the family. You must have concrete Christian marriage again: you can't have solid small property with all this vagabond polygamy; a harem that isn't even a home."

Green nodded and rose slowly to his feet, with his hands in his pockets.

"When it comes to a fight," he said. "When I look at these enormous underground preparations, it is not difficult to infer that you think it will come to a fight."

"I think it has come to a fight," answered Blair. "Lord Eden has decided that. And the others may not understand exactly what they are doing; but he does."

And Blair knocked out his pipe and stood up, to resume his work in that mountain laboratory; at about the same time at which Lord Eden awoke from his smiling meditations and, lighting a cigarette, went languidly indoors.

He did not attempt to explain what was in his mind to the men around him. He was the only man there who understood that the England about him was not the England that had surrounded his youth and supported his leisure and luxury; that things were breaking up, first slowly and then more and more swiftly, and that the things detaching themselves were both good and evil. And one of them was this bald, broad and menacing new fact: a peasantry. The class of small farmers already existed, and might yet be found fighting for its farms like the same class all over the world. It was no longer certain that the sweeping social adjustments settled in that garden could be applied to the whole English land. But the story of how far his doubts were justified, and how far his whole project fared, is a part of the story of The Ultimate Ultimatum of the League of the Long Bow, after which the exhausted and broken-spirited reader may find rest at last.

VIII

The Ultimate Ultimatum of the League of the Long Bow

Mr Robert Owen Hood came through his library that was lined with brown leather volumes with a brown paper parcel in his hand; a flippant person (such as his friend Mr Pierce) might have said he was in a brown study. He came out into the sunlight of his garden, however, where his wife was arranging tea-things, for she was expecting visitors. Even in the strong daylight he looked strangely little altered, despite the long and catastrophic period that had passed since he had met her in the Thames valley and managed really to set the Thames on fire. That fire had since spread in space and time and become a conflagration in which much of modern civilization had been consumed; but in which (as its advocates alleged) English agriculture had been saved and a new and more hopeful chapter opened in English history. His angular face was rather more lined and wrinkled, but his straight shock of copper-coloured hair was as unchanged as if it had been a copper-coloured wig. His wife Elizabeth was even less marked, for she was younger; she had the same slightly nervous or short-sighted look in the eyes that was like a humanizing touch to her beauty made of ivory and gold. But though she was not old she had always been a little old-fashioned; for she came of a forgotten aristocracy whose women had moved with a certain gravity as well as grace about the old country houses, before coronets were sold like cabbages or the Jews lent money to the squires. But her husband was old-fashioned too; though he had just taken part in a successful revolution and bore a revolutionary name, he also had his prejudices; and one of them was a weakness for his wife being a lady – especially that lady.

"Owen," she said, looking up from the tea-table with alarmed severity, "you've been buying more old books."

"As it happens, these are particularly new books," he replied; "but I suppose in one sense it's all ancient history now."

"What ancient history?" she asked. "Is it a History of Babylon or prehistoric China?"

"It is a History of Us."

"I hope not," she said; "but what do you mean?"

"I mean it's a history of Our Revolution," said Owen Hood, "a true and authentic account of the late glorious victories, as the old broadsheets said. The Great War of 1914 started the fashion of bringing out the history of events almost before they'd happened. There were standard histories of that war while it was still going on. Our little civil war is at least finished, thank God; and this is the brand-new history of it. Written by a rather clever fellow, detached but understanding and a little ironical on the right side. Above all, he gives quite a good description of the Battle of the Bows."

"I shouldn't call that our history," said Elizabeth quietly. "I'm devoutly thankful that nobody can ever write our history or put it in a book. Do you remember when you jumped into the water after the flowers? I fancy it was then that you really set the Thames on fire."

"With my red hair, no doubt," he replied; "but I don't think I did set the Thames on fire. I think it was the Thames that set me on fire. Only you were always the spirit of the stream and the goddess of the valley."

"I hope I'm not quite so old as that," answered Elizabeth.

"Listen to this," cried her husband, turning over the pages of the book. " 'According to the general belief, which prevailed until the recent success of the agrarian movement of the Long Bow, it was overwhelmingly improbable that a revolutionary change could be effected in England. The recent success of the agrarian protest – ' "

"Do come out of that book," remonstrated his wife. "One of our visitors has just arrived."

The visitor proved to be the Reverend Wilding White, a man who had also played a prominent part in the recent triumph, a part that was sometimes highly public and almost pontifical; but in private life he had always a way of entering with his grey hair brushed or blown the wrong way and his eagle face eager or indignant; and his conversation like his correspondence came in a rush and was too explosive to be explanatory.

"I say," he cried, "I've come to talk to you about that idea, you know – Enoch Oates wrote about it from America, and he's a jolly good fellow and all that; but after all he does come from America, and so he thinks it's quite easy. But you can see for yourself it isn't quite so easy, what with Turks and all that. It's all very well to talk about the United States – "

"Never you mind about the United States," said Hood easily; "I think I'm rather in favour of the Heptarchy. You just listen to this; the epic of our own Heptarchy, the story of our own dear little domestic war. 'The recent success of the agrarian protest – ' "

He was interrupted again by the arrival of two more guests; by the silent entrance of Colonel Crane and the very noisy entrance of Captain Pierce, who had brought his young wife with him from the country, for they had established themselves in the ancestral inn of the Blue Boar. White's wife was still in the country and Crane's having long been busy in her studio with war posters, was now equally busy with peace posters.

Hood was one of those men whom books almost literally seize and swallow, like monsters with leather or paper jaws. It was no exaggeration to say he was deep in a book as an incautious traveller might be deep in a swamp or some strange man-eating plant of the tropics; only that the traveller was magnetized and did not even struggle. He would fall suddenly silent in the middle of a sentence and go on reading; or he would suddenly begin to read aloud with great passion, arguing with somebody in the book without reference to anybody in the room. Though not normally rude, he would drift through other people's drawing-rooms towards other people's bookshelves and disappear into them, so to speak, like a rusty family ghost. He would travel a hundred miles to see a friend for an hour, and then waste half an hour with his head in some odd volume he never happened to have seen before. On all that side of him there was a sort of almost creepy unconsciousness. His wife, who had old-world notions of the graces of a hostess, sometimes had double work to do.

" 'The recent success of the agrarian protest,' " began Hood cheerfully as his wife rose swiftly to receive two more visitors. These were Professor Green and Commander Bellew Blair; for a queer friendship had long linked together the most practical and the most unpractical of the brothers of the Long Bow. The friendship, as Pierce remarked, was firmly rooted in the square root of minus infinity.

"How beautiful your garden is looking," said Blair to his hostess. "One so seldom sees flower-beds like that now; but I shall always think the old gardeners were right."

"Most things are old-fashioned here, I'm afraid," replied Elizabeth, "but I always like them like that. And how are the children?"

" 'The recent success of the agrarian protest,' " remarked her husband in a clear voice, " 'is doubtless – ' "

"Really," she said, laughing, "you are too ridiculous for anything. Why in the world should you want to read out the history of the war to the people who were in it, and know quite well already what really happened?"

"I beg your pardon," said Colonel Crane. "Very improper to contradict a lady, but indeed you are mistaken. The very last thing the soldier generally knows is what has really happened. Has to look at a newspaper next morning for the realistic description of what never happened."

"Why, then you'd better go on reading, Hood," said Hilary Pierce. "The Colonel wants to know whether he was killed in battle; or whether there was any truth in that story that he was hanged as a spy on the very tree he had climbed when running away as a deserter."

"Should rather like to know what they make of it all," said the Colonel. "After all, we were all too deep in it to see it. I mean see it as a whole."

"If Owen once begins he won't stop for hours," said the lady.

"Perhaps," began Blair, "we had better – "

" 'The recent success of the agrarian protest,' " remarked Hood in authoritative tones, " 'is doubtless to be attributed largely to the economic advantage belonging to an agrarian population. It can feed the town or refuse to feed the town; and this question appeared early in the politics of the peasantry that had arisen in the western counties. Nobody will forget the scene at Paddington Station in the first days of the rebellion. Men who had grown used to seeing on innumerable mornings the innumerable ranks and rows of great milk-cans, looking leaden in a grey and greasy light, found themselves faced with a blank, in which those neglected things shone in the memory like stolen silver. It was true, as Sir Horace Hunter eagerly pointed out when he was put in command of the highly hygienic problem of the milk supply, that there would be no difficulty about manufacturing the metal cans, perhaps even of an improved pattern, with a rapidity and finish of which the rustics of Somerset were quite incapable. He had long been of the opinion, the learned doctor explained, that the shape of the cans, especially the small cans left outside poor houses, left much to be desired, and the whole process of standing these small objects about in the basements of private houses was open to grave objection in the matter of waste of space. The public, however, showed an indifference to this new issue and a disposition to go back on the old demand for milk; in which matter, they said, there was an unfair advantage for the man who possessed a cow over the man who only possessed a can. But the story that Hunter had rivalled the agrarian slogan by proclaiming the policy of 'Three Areas and a Can' was in all probability a flippant invention of his enemies.

" 'These agrarian strikes had already occurred at intervals before they culminated in the agrarian war. They were the result of the attempt to enforce on the farmers certain general regulations and precautions about their daily habit, dress and diet, which Sir Horace Hunter and Professor Hake had found to be of great advantage in the large State laboratories for the manufacture of poisons and destructive gases. There was every reason to believe that the people, especially the young people, of the village often evaded the regulation about the gutta-percha masks, and the rule requiring the worker to paint himself all over with an antiseptic gum: and the sending of inspectors from London to see that these rules were enforced led to lamentable scenes of violence. It would be an error, however, to attribute the whole of this great social convulsion to any local agricultural dispute. The causes must also be sought in the general state of society, especially political society. The Earl of Eden was a statesman of great skill by the old Parliamentary standards, but he was already old when he launched his final defiance to the peasants in the form of Land Nationalization; and the General Election which was the result of this departure fell largely into the hands of his lieutenants like Hunter and Low. It soon became apparent that some of the illusions of the Eden epoch had worn rather thin. It was found that the democracy could not always be intimidated even by the threat of consulting them about the choice of a Government.

" 'Nor can it be denied that the General Election of 19— was from the first rendered somewhat unreal by certain legal fictions which had long been spreading. There was a custom, originating in the harmless and humane deception used upon excited maiden ladies from the provinces, by which the private secretaries of the Prime Minister would present themselves as that politician himself; sometimes completing the innocent illusion by brushing their hair, waxing their moustaches or wearing their eyeglasses in the manner of their master. When this custom was extended to public platforms it cannot be denied that it became more questionable. In the last days of that venerable statesman it has been asserted that there were no less than five Lloyd Georges touring the country at the same time, and that the contemporary Chancellor of the Exchequer had appeared simultaneously in three cities on the same night, while the original of all these replicas, the popular and brilliant Chancellor himself, was enjoying a well-earned rest by the Lake of Como. The incident of two identical Lord Smiths appearing side by side on the same platform (through a miscalculation of the party agents), though received with good humour and honest merriment by the audience, did but little good to the serious credit of parliamentary institutions. There was of course a certain exaggeration in the suggestion of the satirist that a whole column of identical Prime Ministers, walking two and two like soldiers, marched out of Downing Street every morning and distributed themselves to their various posts like policemen; but such satires were popular and widely scattered, especially by an active young gentleman who was the author of most of them – Captain Hilary Pierce, late of the Flying Corps.

" 'But if this was true of such trifles as a half a dozen of Prime Ministers, it was even truer and more trying in the practical matter of party programmes and proposals. The heading of each party programme with the old promise 'Every Man a Millionaire' had of course become merely formal, like a decorative pattern or border. But it cannot be denied that the universal use of this phrase, combined with the equally universal sense of the unfairness of expecting any politician to carry it out, somewhat weakened the force of words in political affairs. It would have been well if statesmen had confined themselves to these accepted and familiar formalities. Unfortunately, under the stress of the struggle which arose out of the menacing organization of the League of the Long Bow, they sought to dazzle their followers with new improbabilities instead of adhering to the tried and trusty improbabilities that had done them yeoman service in the past.

" 'Thus it was unwise of Lord Normantowers, so far to depart from the temperance principles of a lifetime as to promise all his workers a bottle of champagne at every meal, if they would consent to complete the provision of munitions for suppressing the Long Bow rebellion. The great philanthropist unquestionably had the highest intentions, both in his rash promise and his more reasonable fulfilment. But when the munitions-workers found that the champagne bottles, though carefully covered with the most beautiful gold-foil, contained in fact nothing but hygienically boiled water, the result was a sudden and sensational strike, which paralysed the whole output of munitions and led to the first incredible victories of the League of the Long Bow.

" 'There followed in consequence one of the most amazing wars of human history – a one-sided war. One side would have been insignificant if the other had not been impotent. The minority could not have fought for long; only the majority could not fight at all. There prevailed through the whole of the existing organizations of society a universal distrust that turned them into a dust of disconnected atoms. What was the use of offering men higher pay when they did not believe they would ever receive it, but only alluded jeeringly to Lord

Normantowers and his brand of champagne? What was the use of telling every man that he would have a bonus, when you had told him for twenty years that he would soon be a millionaire? What was the good of the Prime Minister pledging his honour in a ringing voice on platform after platform, when it was already an open jest that it was not the Prime Minister at all? The Government voted taxes and they were not paid. It mobilized armies and they did not move. It introduced the pattern of a new all-pulverizing gun, and nobody would make it and nobody would fire it off. We all remember the romantic crisis when no less a genius than Professor Hake came to Sir Horace Hunter, the Minister of Scientific Social Organization, with a new explosive capable of shattering the whole geological formation of Europe and sinking these islands in the Atlantic, but was unable to induce the cabman or any of the clerks to assist him in lifting it out of the cab.

" 'Against all this anarchy of broken promises the little organization of the League of the Long Bow stood solid and loyal and dependable. The Long Bowmen had become popular by the nickname of the Liars. Everywhere the jest or catchword was repeated like a song, 'Only the Liars Tell the Truth.' They found more and more men to work and fight for them, because it was known that they would pay whatever wages they promised, and refuse to promise anything that they could not perform. The nickname became an ironical symbol of idealism and dignity. A man was proud of being a little precise and even pedantic in his accuracy and probity because he was a Liar. The whole of this strange organization had originated in certain wild bets or foolish practical jokes indulged in by a small group of eccentrics. But they had prided themselves on the logical, if rather literal, fashion in which they had fulfilled certain vows about white elephants or flying pigs. Hence, when they came to stand for a policy of peasant proprietorship, and were enabled by the money of an American crank to establish it in a widespread fashion across the west of England, they took the more serious task with the same tenacity. When their foes mocked them with 'the myth of three acres and a cow,' they answered: 'Yes, it is as mythical as the cow that jumped over the moon. But our myths come true.'

" 'The inexplicable and indeed incredible conclusion of the story was due to a new fact; the fact of the actual presence of the new peasantry. They had first come into complete possession of their farms, by the deed of gift signed by Enoch Oates in the February of 19— and had thus been settled on the land a great many years when Lord Eden and his Cabinet finally committed themselves to the scheme of Land Nationalization by which their homesteads were to pass into official control. That curious and inexplicable thing, the spirit of the peasant, had made great strides in the interval. It was found that the Government could not move such people about from place to place, as it is possible to do with the urban poor in the reconstruction of streets or the destruction of slums. It was not a thing like moving pawns, but a thing like pulling up plants; and plants that had already struck their roots very deep. In short, the Government, which had already adopted a policy commonly called Socialist from motives that were in fact very conservative, found itself confronted with the same peasant resistance as brought the Bolshevist Government in Russia to a standstill. And when Lord Eden and his Cabinet put in motion the whole modern machinery of militarism and coercion to crush the little experiment, he found himself confronted with a rural rising such as has not been known in England since the Middle Ages.

" 'It is said that the men of the Long Bow carried their medieval symbolism so far as to wear Lincoln green as their uniform when they retired to the woods in the manner of Robin Hood. It is certain that they did employ the weapon after which they were named; and curiously enough, as will be seen, by no means without effect. But it must be clearly understood that when the new agrarian class took to the woods like outlaws, they did not feel in the least like robbers. They hardly even felt like rebels. From their point of view at least, they were and had long been the lawful owners of their own fields, and the officials who came to confiscate were the robbers. Therefore when Lord Eden proclaimed Nationalization, they turned out in thousands as their fathers would have gone out against pirates or wolves.

" 'The Government acted with great promptitude. It instantly voted £50,000 to Mr Rosenbaum Low, the expenditure of which was wisely left to his discretion at so acute a crisis, with no more than the understanding that he should take a thorough general survey of the situation. He proved worthy of the trust; and it was with the gravest consideration and sense of responsibility that he selected Mr Leonard Kramp, the brilliant young financier, from all his other nephews to take command of the forces in the field. In the field, however, fortune is well known to be somewhat more incalculable; and all the intelligence and presence of mind that had enabled Kramp to postpone the rush on the Potosi Bank were not sufficient to balance the accidental possession by Crane and Pierce of an elementary knowledge of strategy.

" 'Before considering the successes obtained by these commanders in the rather rude fashion of warfare which they were forced to adopt, it must be noted, of course, that even on their side there were also scientific resources of a kind; and an effective if eccentric kind. The scientific genius of Bellew Blair had equipped his side with many secret processes affecting aviation and aeronautics, and it is the peculiarity of this extraordinary man that his secret processes really remained for a considerable time secret. For he had not told them to anybody with any intention of making any money out of them. This quixotic and visionary behaviour contrasted sharply with the shrewd good sense of the great business men who know that publicity is the soul of business. For some time past they had successfully ignored the outworn sentimental prejudice that had prevented soldiers and sailors from advertising the best methods of defeating the enemy; and we can all recall those brilliantly coloured announcements which used to brighten so many hoardings in those days, 'Sink in Smith's Submarine; Pleasure Trips for Patriots.' Or 'Duffin's Portable Dug-Out Makes War a Luxury.' Advertisement cannot fail to effect its aim; the name of an aeroplane that had been written on the sky in pink and pea-green lights could not but become a symbol of the conquest of the air; and the patriotic statesman, deeply considering what sort of battleship might best defend his country's coasts, was insensibly and subtly influenced by the number of times that he had seen its name repeated on the steps of a moving staircase at an Imperial Exhibition. Nor could there be any doubt about the brilliant success that attended these scientific specialties so long as their operations were confined to the market. The methods of Commander Blair were in comparison private, local, obscure and lacking any general recognition; and by a strange irony it was a positive advantage to this nameless and secretive crank that he had never advertised his weapons until he used them. He had paraded a number of merely fanciful balloons and fireworks for a jest; but the secrets to which he attached importance he had hidden in cracks of the Welsh mountains with a curious and callous indifference to the principles of commercial distribution and display He could not in any case have conducted operations on a large scale, being deficient in that capital, the lack of which has so often been fatal to inventors; and had made it useless for a man to discover a machine unless he could also discover a millionaire. But it cannot be denied that when his machine was brought into operation it was always operative, even to the point of killing the millionaire who might have financed it. For the millionaire had so persistently cultivated the virtues of self-advertisement that it was difficult for him to become suddenly unknown and undistinguished, even in scenes of conflict where he most ardently desired to do so. There was a movement on foot for treating all millionaires as non-combatants, as being treasures belonging alike to all nations, like the Cathedrals or the Parthenon. It is said that there was even an alternative scheme for camouflaging the millionaire by the pictorial methods that can disguise a gun as a part of the landscape; and that Captain Pierce devoted much eloquence to persuading Mr Rosenbaum Low how much better it would be for all parties if his face could be made to melt away into the middle distance or take on the appearance of a blank wall or a wooden post.' "

"The extraordinary thing is," interrupted Pierce, who had been listening eagerly, "that he said I was personal. Just at the moment when I was trying to make him most impersonal, when I was trying to wave away all personal features that could come between us, he actually said I was personal."

Hood went on reading as if nobody had spoken.

" 'In truth the successes of Blair's instruments revealed a fallacy in the common commercial argument. We talk of a competition between two kinds of soap or two kinds of jam or cocoa, but it is a competition in purchase and not in practice. We do not make two men eat two kinds of jam and then observe which wears the most radiant smile of satisfaction. We do not give two men two kinds of cocoa and note which endures it with most resignation. But we do use two guns directly against each other; and in the case of Blair's methods the less advertised gun was the better. Nevertheless his scientific genius could only cover a corner of the field; and a great part of the war must be considered as a war in the open country of a much more primitive and sometimes almost prehistoric kind.

" 'It is admitted of course by all students that the victories of Crane and Pierce were gross violations of strategic science. The victors themselves afterwards handsomely acknowledged the fact; but it was then too late to repair the error. In order to understand it, however, it is necessary to grasp the curious condition into which so many elements of social life had sunk in the time just preceding the outbreak. It was this strange social situation which rendered the campaign a contradiction to so many sound military maxims.

" 'For instance, it is a recognized military maxim that armies depend upon roads. But anyone who had noticed the conditions that were already beginning to appear in the London streets as early as 1924 will understand that a road was something less simple and static than the Romans imagined. The Government had adopted everywhere in their road-making the well-known material familiar to us all from the advertisements by the name of "Nobumpo," thereby both insuring the comfort of travellers and rewarding a faithful supporter by placing a large order with Mr Hugg. As several members of the Government themselves held shares in Nobumpo their enthusiastic co-operation in the public work was assured. But, as has no doubt been observed everywhere, it is one of the many advantages of Nobumpo, as preserving that freshness of surface so agreeable to the pedestrian, that the whole material can be (and is) taken up and renewed every three months, for the comfort of travellers and the profit and encouragement of trade. It so happened that at the precise moment of the outbreak of hostilities all the country roads, especially in the west, were as completely out of use as if they had been the main thoroughfares of London. This in itself tended to equalize the chances or even to increase them in favour of a guerilla force, such as that which had disappeared into the woods and was everywhere moving under cover of the trees. Under modern conditions, it was found that by carefully avoiding roads, it was still more or less possible to move from place to place.

" 'Again, another recognized military fact is the fact that the bow is an obsolete weapon. And nothing is more irritating to a finely balanced taste than to be killed with an obsolete weapon, especially while persistently pulling the trigger of an efficient weapon, without any apparent effect. Such was the fate of the few unfortunate regiments which ventured to advance into the forests and fell under showers of arrows from trackless ambushes. For it must be remembered that the conditions of this extraordinary campaign entirely reversed the normal military rule about the essential military department of supply. Mechanical communications theoretically accelerate supply, while the supply of a force cut loose and living on the country is soon exhausted. But the mechanical factor also depends upon a moral factor. Ammunition would on normal occasions have been produced with unequalled rapidity by Poole's Process and brought up with unrivalled speed in Blinker's Cars; but not at the moment when riotous employees were engaged in dipping Poole repeatedly in a large vat at the factory; or in the quieter conditions of the countryside, where various tramps were acquiring squatter's rights in Blinker's Cars, accidentally delayed upon their journey. Everywhere the same thing happened; just as the great manufacturer failed to keep his promise to the workers who produced munitions, so the petty officials driving the lorries had failed to keep their promises to loafers and vagrants who had helped them out of temporary difficulties; and the whole system of supply broke down upon a broken word. On the other hand, the supply of the outlaws was in a sense almost infinite. With the woodcutters and the blacksmiths on their side, they could produce their own rude medieval weapons everywhere. It was in vain that Professor Hake delivered a series of popular lectures, proving to the lower classes that in the long run it would be to their economic advantage to be killed in battle. Captain Pierce is reported to have said: 'I believe the Professor is a botanist as well as an economist; but as a botanist he has not yet discovered that guns do not grow on trees. Bows and arrows do.'

" 'But the incident which history will have most difficulty in explaining, and which it may perhaps refer to the region of myth or romance, is the crowning victory commonly called the Battle of the Bows. It was indeed originally called 'The Battle of the Bows of God'; in reference to some strangely fantastic boast, equally strangely fulfilled, that is said to have been uttered by the celebrated Parson White, a sort of popular chaplain who seems to have been the Friar Tuck of this new band of Robin Hood. Coming on a sort of embassy to Sir Horace Hunter, this clergyman is said to have threatened the Government with something like a miracle. When rallied about the archaic sport of the long bow, he replied: 'Yes, we have long bows and we shall have longer bows; the longest bows the world has ever seen; bows taller than houses; bows given to us by God Himself and big enough for His gigantic angels.'

" 'The whole business of this battle, historic and decisive as it was, is covered with some obscurity, like that cloud of storm that hung heavy upon the daybreak of that gloomy November day. Had anyone been present with the Government forces who was well acquainted with the western valley in which they were operating, such a person could not have failed to notice that the very landscape looked different; looked new and abnormal. Dimly as it could be traced through the morning twilight, the very line of the woodland against the sky would have shown him a new shape; a deformity like a hump. But the plans had all been laid out in London long before, in imitation of that foresight, fixity of purpose, and final success that will always be associated with the last German Emperor. It was enough for them that there was a wood of some sort marked on the map, and they advanced towards it, low and crouching as its entrance appeared to be.

" 'Then something happened, which even those who saw it and survived cannot describe. The dark trees seemed to spring up to twice their height as in a nightmare. In the half-dark the whole wood seemed to rise from the earth like a rush of birds and then to turn over in mid-air and come towards the invaders like a roaring wave. Some such dim and dizzy sight they saw; but many of them at least saw little enough afterwards. Simultaneously with the turning of this wheel of waving trees, rocks seemed to rain down out of heaven; beams and stones and shafts and missiles of all kinds, flattening out the advancing force as under a pavement produced by a shower of paving-stones. It is asserted that some of the countrymen cunning in woodcraft, in the service of the Long Bow, had contrived to fit up a tree as a colossal catapult; calculating how to bend back the boughs and sometimes even the trunks to the breaking-point, and gaining a huge and living resilience with their release. If this story is true, it is certainly an appropriate conclusion to the career of the Long Bow and a rather curious fulfilment of the visionary vaunt of Parson White, when he said that the bows would be big enough for giants, and that the maker of the bows was God.' "

"Yes," interrupted the excitable White, "and do you know what he said to me when I first said it?"

"What who said when you said what?" asked Hood patiently.

"I mean that fellow Hunter," replied the clergyman. "That varnished society doctor turned politician. Do you know what he said when I told him we would get our bows from God?"

Owen Hood paused in the act of lighting a cigar.

"Yes," he said grimly. "I believe I can tell you exactly what he said. I've watched him off and on for twenty years. I bet he began by saying: 'I don't profess to be a religious man.' "

"Right, quite right," cried the cleric bounding upon his chair in a joyous manner, "that's exactly how he began. 'I don't profess to be a religious man, but I trust I have some reverence and good taste. I don't drag religion into politics.' And I said: 'No, I don't think you do.' "

A moment after, he bounded, as it were, in a new direction. "And that reminds me of what I came about," he cried. "Enoch Oates, your American friend, drags religion into politics all right; only it's a rather American sort of religion. He's talking about a United States of Europe and wants to introduce you to a Lithuanian Prophet. It seems this Lithuanian party has started a movement for a Universal Peasant Republic or World State of Workers on the Land; but at present he's only got as far as

Lithuania. But he seems inclined to pick up England on the way, after the unexpected success of the English agrarian party."

"What's the good of talking to me about a World State," growled Hood. "Didn't I say I preferred a Heptarchy?"

"Don't you understand?" interrupted Hilary Pierce excitedly. "What can we have to do with international republics? We can turn England upside down if we like; but it's England that we like, whichever way up. Why, our very names and phrases, the very bets and jokes in which the whole thing began, will never be translated. It takes an Englishman to eat his hat; I never heard of a Spaniard threatening to eat his sombrero, or a Chinaman to chew his pigtail. You can only set the Thames on fire; you cannot set the Tiber or the Ganges on fire, because the habit of speech has never been heard of. What's the good of talking about white elephants in countries where they are only white elephants? Go and say to a Frenchman, '*Pour mon château, je le trouve un éléphant blanc*' and he will send two Parisian alienists to look at you seriously, like a man who says that his motor car is a green giraffe. There is no point in telling Czecho-Slovakian pigs to fly or Jugo-Slavonic cows to jump over the moon. Why the unhappy Lithuanian would be bewildered to the point of madness by our very name. There is no reason to suppose that he and his countrymen talk about a long bowman when they mean a liar. We talk about tall stories, but a tall story may mean a true story in colloquial Lithuanian."

"Tall stories are true stories sometimes, I hope," said Colonel Crane, "and people don't believe 'em. But people'll say that was a very tall story about the tall trees throwing darts and stones. Afraid it'll come to be a bit of a joke."

"All our battles began as jokes and they will end as jokes," said Owen Hood, staring at the smoke of his cigar as it threaded its way towards the sky in grey and silver arabesque. "They will linger only as faintly laughable legends, if they linger at all; they may pass an hour or two or fill an empty page; and even the man who tells them will not take them seriously. It will all end in smoke like the smoke I am looking at; in eddying and topsy-turvy patterns hovering for a moment in the air. And I wonder how many, who may smile or yawn over them, will realize that where there was smoke there was fire."

There was a silence; then Colonel Crane stood up, a solitary figure in his severe and formal clothes, and gravely said farewell to his hostess. With the failing afternoon light he knew that his own wife, who was a well-known artist, would be abandoning her studio work, and he always looked forward to a talk with her before dinner, which was often a more social function. Nevertheless, as he approached his old home a whim induced him to delay the meeting for a few minutes and to walk round to his old kitchen garden, where his old servant Archer was still leaning on a spade, as in the days before the Flood.

So he stood for a moment amid a changing world, exactly as he had stood on that distant Sunday morning at the beginning of all these things. The South Sea idol still stood at the corner; the scarecrow still wore the hat that he had sacrificed; the cabbages still looked green and solid like the cabbage he had once dug up, digging up so much along with it.

"Queer thing," he said, "how true it is what Hilary once said about acting an allegory without knowing it. Never had a notion of what I was doing when I picked up a cabbage and wore it for a wager. Damned awkward position, but I never dreamed I was being martyred for a symbol. And the right symbol, too, for I've lived to see Britannia crowned with cabbage. All very well to say Britannia ruled the waves; it was the land she couldn't rule, her own land, and it was heaving like earthquakes. But while there's cabbage there's hope. Archer, my friend, this is the moral: any country that tries to do without cabbages is done for. And even in war you often fight as much with cabbages as cannon-balls."

"Yes, sir," said Archer respectfully; "would you be wanting another cabbage now, sir?"

Colonel Crane repressed a slight shudder. "No, thank you; no, thank you," he said hastily. Then he muttered as he turned away: "I don't mind revolutions so much, but I wouldn't go through that again."

And he passed swiftly round his house, of which the windows began to show the glow of kindled lamps, and went in to his wife.

Archer was left alone in the garden, tidying up after his work and shifting the potted shrubs; a dark and solitary figure as sunset and twilight sank all around the enclosure like soft curtains of grey with a border of purple; and the windows, as yet uncurtained and full of lamplight, painted patterns of gold on the lawns and flagged walks without. It was perhaps appropriate that he should remain alone and apart; for he alone in all these changes had remained quite unchanged. It was perhaps fitting that his figure should stand in a dark outline against the darkening scene; for the mystery of his immutable respectability remains more of a riddle than all the riot of the rest. No revolution could revolutionize Mr Archer. Attempts had been made to provide so excellent a gardener with a garden of his own; with a farm of his own, in accordance with the popular policy of the hour. But he would not adapt himself to the new world; nor would he hasten to die out, as was his duty on evolutionary principles. He was merely a survival; but he showed a perplexing disposition to survive.

Suddenly the lonely gardener realized that he was not alone. A face had appeared above the hedge, gazing at him with blue eyes dreaming yet burning; a face with something of the tint and profile of Shelley. It was impossible that Mr Archer should have heard of such a person as Shelley: fortunately he recognized the visitor as a friend of his master.

"Forgive me if I am mistaken, Citizen Archer," said Hilary Pierce with pathetic eagerness, "but it seems to me that you are not swept along with the movement; that a man of your abilities has been allowed to stand apart, as it were, from the campaign of the Long Bow. And yet how strange! Are you not Archer? Does not your very name rise up and reproach you? Ought you not to have shot more arrows or told more tarradiddles than all the rest? Or is there perhaps a more elemental mystery behind your immobility, like that of a statue in the garden? Are you indeed the god of the garden, more beautiful than this South Sea idol and more respectable than Priapus? Are you in no mortal sense an Archer? Are you perhaps Apollo, serving this military Admetus; successfully, yes, successfully hiding your radiance from me?" He paused for a reply and then lowered his voice as he resumed: "Or are you not rather that other Archer whose shafts are not shafts of death but of life and fruitfulness; whose arrows plant themselves like little flowering trees; like the little shrubs you are planting in this garden? Are you he that gives the sunstroke not in the head but the heart; and have you stricken each of us in turn with the romance that has awakened us for the revolution? For without that spirit of fruitfulness and the promise of the family, these visions would indeed be vain. Are you in truth the God of Love; and has your arrow stung and startled each of us into telling his story? I will not call you Cupid," he said with a slight air of deprecation or apology, "I will not call you Cupid, Mr Archer, for I conceive you as no pagan deity, but rather as that image clarified and spiritualized to a symbol almost Christian, as he might have appeared to Chaucer or to Botticelli. Nay it was you that, clad in no heathen colours, but rather in medieval heraldry blew a blast on his golden trumpet when Beatrice saluted Dante on the bridge. Are you indeed that Archer, O Archer, and did you give each one of us his Vita Nuova?"

"No, sir," said Mr Archer.

Thus does the chronicler of the League of the Long Bow come to the end of his singularly unproductive and unprofitable labours, without, perhaps, having yet come to the beginning. The reader may have once hoped, perhaps, that the story would be like the universe; which when it ends, will explain why it ever began. But the reader has long since been sleeping, after the toils and trials of his part in the affair; and the writer is too tactful to ask at how early a stage of his storytelling that generally satisfactory solution of all our troubles was found. He knows not if the sleep has been undisturbed, or in that sleep what dreams may come, if there has been cast upon it any shadow of the shapes in his own very private and comfortable nightmare; turrets clad with the wings of morning or temples marching over dim meadows as living monsters, or swine plumed like cherubim or forests bent like bows, or a fiery river winding through a dark land. Images are in their nature indefensible, if they miss the imagination of another; and the foolish scribe of the Long Bow will not commit the last folly of defending his dreams. He at least has drawn a bow at a venture and shot an arrow into the air; and he has no intention of looking for it in oaks, all over the neighbourhood, or expecting to find it still sticking in a mortal and murderous manner in the heart of a friend. His is only a toy bow; and when a boy shoots with such a bow, it is generally very difficult to find the arrow – or the boy.

GK Chesterton

The Ball and the Cross

Evan MacIan is a passionate and fiery young Catholic. He is outraged one day by an editorial he reads in The Atheist and vents his anger by smashing the window of the paper's office. He then challenges the editor, Turnbull, to a duel.

The feuding men are thwarted at every turn in their attempt to find a suitable place for their fight. While the search goes on they continue their theological debate. They eventually arrive at a position of acceptance and mutual understanding before the story reaches its powerful conclusion.

The Ballad of the White Horse

This epic poem about King Alfred's defeat of the Danes is full of the colour and the romance of the legend – the Crusades, the Vale of the White Horse and, of course, the Burning of the Cakes. This popular tale is immediately brought to life in what must surely be one of Chesterton's masterpieces.

GK Chesterton

The Man Who Knew Too Much

Horne Fisher is the man who knew too much. He has a brilliant mind and powers of deduction – but he always faces a moral dilemma. These eight adventures will amaze and delight as we follow Horne and his friend, Harold March in the world of crime among eminent people.

The Man Who Was Thursday

Lucian Gregory and Gabriel Syme both dress as poets. In this disturbing fantasy, one is an Anarchist and the other is a policeman. In the surreal anarchist world they inhabit one of them is voted onto the Anarchists' Council of Days and becomes 'Thursday'.

The Nightmare has just begun…

GK Chesterton

The Paradoxes of Mr Pond

Mr Pond was a small, neat civil servant. There was nothing remarkable about him at all – except a pointed beard. However, he tells the most fascinating stories and has the most unorthodox way of solving crimes and mysteries.
These eight short stories include the extraordinary *'The Three Horsemen of the Apocalypse'* about a Marshal's plans which go tragically wrong because, paradoxically, his soldiers obey him.

The Return of Don Quixote

Michael Herne is a gentle, unassuming librarian. When he is asked to play a king in a medieval play he reluctantly agrees. After the play is over, however, strange things begin to happen. Michael refuses to change back into his everyday clothes and other actors find it impossible to return to their real character. Set in the early 20th Century, this is the intriguing story of the rise of a new Don Quixote who introduces a medieval government into the world of big business.

OTHER TITLES BY G K CHESTERTON AVAILABLE DIRECT FROM HOUSE OF STRATUS

Quantity		£	$(US)	$(CAN)	€
	BIOGRAPHY:				
☐	AUTOBIOGRAPHY	8.99	14.99	19.49	15.00
☐	CHARLES DICKENS	8.99	14.99	19.49	15.00
☐	CHAUCER	8.99	14.99	19.49	15.00
☐	CRITICISMS AND APPRECIATIONS OF THE WORKS OF CHARLES DICKENS	8.99	14.99	19.49	15.00
☐	GEORGE BERNARD SHAW	8.99	14.99	19.49	15.00
☐	ROBERT BROWNING	8.99	14.99	19.49	15.00
☐	ROBERT LOUIS STEVENSON	8.99	14.99	19.49	15.00
☐	ST FRANCIS OF ASSISI	8.99	14.99	19.49	15.00
☐	ST THOMAS AQUINAS	8.99	14.99	19.49	15.00
☐	WILLIAM BLAKE	8.99	14.99	19.49	15.00
☐	WILLIAM COBBETT	8.99	14.99	19.49	15.00

OTHER TITLES BY G K CHESTERTON AVAILABLE DIRECT FROM HOUSE OF STRATUS

Quantity		£	$(US)	$(CAN)	€
	GENERAL FICTION:				
☐	THE BALL AND THE CROSS	6.99	11.50	15.99	11.50
☐	THE BALLAD OF THE WHITE HORSE	6.99	11.50	15.99	11.50
☐	THE INCREDULITY OF FATHER BROWN	6.99	11.50	15.99	11.50
☐	THE INNOCENCE OF FATHER BROWN	6.99	11.50	15.99	11.50
☐	THE MAN WHO KNEW TOO MUCH	6.99	11.50	15.99	11.50
☐	THE MAN WHO WAS THURSDAY	6.99	11.50	15.99	11.50
☐	MANALIVE	6.99	11.50	15.99	11.50
☐	THE NAPOLEON OF NOTTING HILL	6.99	11.50	15.99	11.50
☐	THE PARADOXES OF MR POND	6.99	11.50	15.99	11.50
☐	THE POET AND THE LUNATICS	6.99	11.50	15.99	11.50
☐	THE RETURN OF DON QUIXOTE	6.99	11.50	15.99	11.50
☐	THE SCANDAL OF FATHER BROWN	6.99	11.50	15.99	11.50
☐	THE SECRET OF FATHER BROWN	6.99	11.50	15.99	11.50
☐	THE WISDOM OF FATHER BROWN	6.99	11.50	15.99	11.50
	OTHER WORKS:				
☐	HERETICS	8.99	14.99	19.49	15.00
☐	ORTHODOXY	8.99	14.99	19.49	15.00
☐	THE VICTORIAN AGE IN LITERATURE	8.99	14.99	19.49	15.00
☐	WINE, WATER AND SONG	6.99	11.50	15.99	11.50

ALL HOUSE OF STRATUS BOOKS ARE AVAILABLE FROM GOOD BOOKSHOPS OR DIRECT FROM THE PUBLISHER:

Hotline: UK ONLY: 0800 169 1780, please quote author, title and credit card details.
INTERNATIONAL: +44 (0) 20 7494 6400, please quote author, title, and credit card details.

Send to: **House of Stratus Sales Department**
24c Old Burlington Street
London
W1X 1RL
UK

Please allow for postage costs charged per order plus an amount per book as set out in the tables below:

	£(Sterling)	$(US)	$(CAN)	€(Euros)
Cost per order				
UK	2.00	3.00	4.50	3.30
Europe	3.00	4.50	6.75	5.00
North America	3.00	4.50	6.75	5.00
Rest of World	3.00	4.50	6.75	5.00
Additional cost per book				
UK	0.50	0.75	1.15	0.85
Europe	1.00	1.50	2.30	1.70
North America	2.00	3.00	4.60	3.40
Rest of World	2.50	3.75	5.75	4.25

PLEASE SEND CHEQUE, POSTAL ORDER (STERLING ONLY), EUROCHEQUE, OR INTERNATIONAL MONEY ORDER (PLEASE CIRCLE METHOD OF PAYMENT YOU WISH TO USE)
MAKE PAYABLE TO: STRATUS HOLDINGS plc

Cost of book(s): ______ Example: 3 x books at £6.99 each: £20.97
Cost of order: ______ Example: £2.00 (Delivery to UK address)
Additional cost per book: ______ Example: 3 x £0.50: £1.50
Order total including postage: ______ Example: £24.47

Please tick currency you wish to use and add total amount of order:

☐ £ (Sterling) ☐ $ (US) ☐ $ (CAN) ☐ € (EUROS)

VISA, MASTERCARD, SWITCH, AMEX, SOLO, JCB:

☐☐☐☐☐☐☐☐☐☐☐☐☐☐☐☐☐☐☐☐

Issue number (Switch only):

☐☐☐

Start Date: ☐☐/☐☐

Expiry Date: ☐☐/☐☐

Signature: ______

NAME: ______

ADDRESS: ______

______

POSTCODE: ______

Please allow 28 days for delivery.

Prices subject to change without notice.
Please tick box if you do not wish to receive any additional information. ☐

House of Stratus publishes many other titles in this genre; please check our website (**www.houseofstratus.com**) for more details.